Grace

A novel by

Todd Blair

DEDICATION

Based on actual events, many people have had a hand in getting this story to publication.

FOR LEXI!

Thank you all very much!

Chapter One

   In a life full of nightmares, Grace was just hours away from fulfilling another dream.   Starting up the winding trail leading to the summit of Clingmans Dome, with tired aching legs, she lifted her heavy boot to the next log put there by the skilled hands of the Appalachian Trail Club volunteers.   Staring up the steep inclined trail, she knew then what the intense training was for during those rain soaked practice hikes and the short day trips carrying her backpack full of gear in the sweltering southern sunshine.   Now all the training and preparation were paying off.

   Unlike any other woman you would ever hope to meet, her radiant natural beauty made many men and some women blush as if their impure thoughts were being published across their foreheads.   Shimmering red hair and a complexion as smooth as silk stockings, always unassuming, always the generous donor of compliments and kind words, she was the one who brought the homeless warm blankets and dinner.   She never met a soul she didn't like, but she wasn't always like this.

   There was a time some years ago, at the age of 19, when young women should be dancing the night away and dreaming of romance, that a monster of a man was lurking in the shadows watching and waiting for the moment to strike at the innocence she held in her heart.

   It was a late wintery afternoon in February.   The air was cold and blustery, and the sky was a threatening gray aching to blanket the ground with snow.   This was a day that would change the lives of many in the little southern town of Burlington; a small, yet proud and independent place where everybody knew your name and news traveled fast, especially bad.

   Grace was at the library.   She was studying after a night class in biology.   She was enrolled in a pilot program that taught extra credit courses in her related studies.   She was attending North Carolina State University full time in the city.   She was doing well in her studies maintaining a high grade point average with hopes of fulfilling her ambition of becoming a marine biologist.

Classes had ended hours before, but she was too busy researching for an upcoming exam to notice the time.   Suddenly she heard a door slam from a distant room down the hall.   It startled her and caused her to look to the clock on the wall.

"Oh no!   I'm going to be late for dinner," she said aloud as she collected her books and prepared to head home.

As she entered the long corridor towards the front door, she came across the custodian; an old man whom she knew lived out in the back hills of town.   "How are you doing tonight Mr. Shade?" asked Grace.

With a polite smile that turned all the wrinkles on his face into a map of the Grand Canyon, the old man replied, "I couldn't be more blessed; every day I awake is a blessing.   Jesus is always with me.   Are you in a hurry, Miss Grace?"

"Oh yes, Mr. Shade.   Momma is going kill me.   I had no idea it was so late.   I have got to get home quickly before they come looking for me," she answered.

"It looks like it is going to snow some tonight.   You should take your time driving if you want to get there in one piece," he said.

"Amen Mr. Shade, Amen." said Grace, and she wished him a good night and a safe trip home.

"I wish you the same," said the old man.

As she headed to her car in the parking lot, she could feel the uneasy cold that swirled in the wind about her.   Her powder blue Camaro was parked around a cluster of pickup trucks and a U-haul rental truck.   As she approached her car, she reached into her coat pocket and began digging for

2

her keys.   No sooner did she look down to insert the key in the lock when it happened--the moment that changed everything.

In an instant, he was upon her knocking her to the ground.   Grace gasped for the air that the sudden impact had flushed from her lungs.   As she opened her eyes the world closed in around her. For a second, the surreal scene seemed like an accident or a prank by a fellow student.   The scene became very real when the cold steel of a ten inch hunting knife slid across her throat and the horrifying whisper of a serial rapist echoed in her ear demanding her silence and obedience, or else she would pay the ultimate penalty.

Seconds seemed like hours as she lay back on the frozen blacktop, mustering up the strength as she begged, "Please don't hurt me!"

His reply was as cold as the steel on her neck.   "Shut up and do what I say or I will end your life right here and now!   Open your legs."

As she lay motionless, he groped and grabbed at her, squeezing her breasts with his free hand.   Soon he was aroused like a pack of wolves in a feeding frenzy.   She was wearing a long winter dress that her mother had given her for Christmas that year, and her overcoat was from the Christmas a year before.   She loved the warmth it gave her against the winters chill, but now her dress and coat were bunched up around her waist.   He was grabbing and pulling at her panties, tearing and scratching at her flesh as he ripped them off.   Grace was bruised and bleeding from the scrapes on her knees and as he slid his hand between her thighs.   Her instincts took over, and she tried to close her legs tight, but he was stronger than she was, and the knife grew tighter against her throat.

Suddenly he stopped, and she thought for an instant it was over, but he was only switching hands on the knife and suddenly she felt him.   He was rigid and hot against her thigh, and the horrible terror of what was about to happen consumed her.   She felt herself turn inward into a place in her mind she never knew existed.

The further he pushed into her, the deeper she retreated to that safe place in her mind until she was oblivious to what was happening to her. Time stood still for those brief moments, and when he was through, he slid the knife across her throat and pressed the tip under her chin, making her promise to never tell or he would kill her.

As he got up and fixed his pants and belt, he looked down at her as she began to sob.   He told her he had been watching her for weeks, and he knew where she lived.   She promised him her silence if he let her go, and with that, he ran off, disappearing behind the rental truck from where he had come.   As she rose to her feet, her knees were shaking. Her hands were stiff and cold.   She didn't notice her dress was nearly torn off as she turned to look for help.   She started to run for home leaving behind her car with her coat on the ground beside it.

Grace was the kind of daughter who didn't want her parents to worry about her. She always informed them if she was going to be late.   It was her father who noticed her absence first, and since Grace was a girl who kept her word, he decided to take a ride to the school to see if she had left.

An auto mechanic, Grace's dad was a simple man, a man of few words, but when he spoke his words were to the point and often prophetic.   He loved his family and worked hard to provide a safe and comfortable home life in small town in America.

Perhaps he felt something was wrong in his heart, because he took a different route to the school than was normal.   As he rounded the corner, he caught sight of the school and at the same time saw his worst fears come true.

There was his baby girl overwhelmed with tears, half-naked with her dress torn exposing her body to the frigid winter weather.   Blood was visibly streaming down her shins from the scrapes on her knees. Handprints were still plainly visible about her shivering body, reminders left by her brutal assailant.

When Grace saw her daddy's truck, any self-control she had left escaped as she became hysterical.   Zachary Fields screeched his truck to

4

an abrupt halt in the middle of the road and ran to his distressed daughter. He carried her to the truck, and in an instant he knew what had happened and what he needed to do.

Grace began to scream incoherently as he sped down the road towards home; all the while he was begging her to calm down and tell him who did it.

When they arrived home, Susan, Grace's mom, was in the kitchen preparing dinner for her family. She had no idea that her life was about to be turned upside down. Alex, Grace's younger brother, who was barely a teenager, was upstairs doing his homework when he heard all the commotion and came downstairs to investigate. When he arrived in the kitchen, Grace was wrapped in a blanket while Susan was wiping her face with a warm damp cloth. As the tears were wiped from her eyes she began to calm and let the safety of her familiar surroundings sink inside her heart.

"He had a knife at my throat, Momma! What was I supposed to do? I didn't want him to hurt me, but I couldn't stop him!"

Susan squeezed Grace tightly and told her it wasn't her fault; she did nothing wrong, nothing to deserve this.

Grace cried, "He knows where I live; he said he would kill me if I reported it!"

Susan looked in her daughter's eyes and said, "We will not let anything happen to you. I promise we will protect you, but Grace we have to get you to a doctor and get you checked over. Your dad's on the phone with the Sheriff's Department; he is trying to find out what we should do first."

"Please, Momma!" Grace begged. "Don't call the police. Please don't. I don't want to go through this anymore!"

Susan sighed and said with a sympathetic insistence, "Grace, if we do nothing then the next girl might not get away." Grace began to cry as she buried her head and face into her momma's shoulder.

Her dad came back from the bedroom and said, "The Sheriff's Deputy is sending someone over who will go with us to the hospital so they can collect evidence and check Grace out."

When Grace heard the word evidence, she knew right away it meant her. It was then and there that she changed. She straightened up and took a deep breath, just like back in high school when she ran on the track team. Looking at her mom and dad, seeing the immense strain that was already evident on their faces, she dug down deep within and said, "Okay, okay, I will go to the hospital. I will report the rape and I will do whatever it takes to make the son of a bitch, monster pay!"

Deputy Miller was standing in the waiting room at the hospital when Grace arrived. He was a stalky, muscular man, of average height. He had chocolate brown eyes; his light brown hair was kept short above his ears. He was wearing a Sherriff's cap and uniform--he was very handsome.

She was clearly upset and clinging to her mom. She was still wrapped in a woolen blanket and Zachary was carrying a small travel bag. Deputy Miller a five-year veteran officer had seen a few rape cases in his time and he knew they were hard to investigate. Most of the victims were never the same and some of the rapists were never convicted. As Grace got closer Deputy Miller reminded himself not to get emotionally involved. He learned early on that police work was difficult enough. You had to keep your distance from each case or you would have many sleepless nights.

Deputy Miller approached Zachary Fields and held out his hand to introduce himself. "How are you all doing tonight?" asked the Deputy. No one said a word, so he turned and pointed to a door off to the side of the lobby and asked them to follow him. He led them into the small private waiting room and invited them to sit down.

Against the back wall, next to another door labeled Exam Room 1, there was a small desk with two chairs on either side. Deputy Miller laid a folder on the desk and turned to look at Grace.   He stared at her for a moment and then caught himself, realizing what he was doing.   He suddenly became shy and embarrassed for himself.   Without looking at her, he asked if she was ready to go in and see the doctor.

"Yes." she said, she turned and looked at Susan. "Momma, will you come with me?"

"Oh, yes, of course," said Susan.

Deputy Miller went over and knocked on the exam room door.   A moment later, a heavyset black woman entered the room.   She smiled reassuringly at Grace as she put her arm around her shoulder.   "C'mon honey.   My name is Nurse Grainger, but everybody calls me Kay.   Are you ready to come in and let Dr. Cooke examine you?"

Grace hesitated and then nodded as she allowed Nurse Kay to lead her into the examination room.

Deputy Miller looked at Zachary and said, "Mr. Fields, I am so very sorry this happened to your daughter.   We'll find the son-of-a-bitch who did this to her, I promise.   Let's get to work right away and start looking for this guy.   Is there any new information since we spoke on the phone?"

Zachary leaned back in his chair; he could feel the sweat on his brow and chills went up his spine as he thought about what the Deputy had just asked.   His little girl had just been brutally assaulted.   Now they all had to relive the experience again.   After telling the Deputy in detail everything he could remember, Deputy Miller suggested the two men take a break and go for a coffee in the cafeteria.

"Is it smoking or non-smoking?" asked Zachary.   "I really need a cigarette right now."

"The entire hospital is non-smoking," replied Deputy Miller, "but we can go outside, and you can smoke out there all you like."

"I may need to get a new pack if this takes too long." said Zachary.

"They shouldn't be too much longer," said Deputy Miller. "It all depends on the seriousness of Grace's injuries, and I don't think she's in too bad of shape physically. We should have you folks on your way soon. In the morning, we will be going over to the crime scene. I will need to meet you there at 8:30 a.m. We have deputies on the scene now. The area has been taped off, and we are looking for any possible witnesses."

For the next few minutes, Zachary and Deputy Miller spoke in a casual manner not related to Grace. Zachary told of his garage in town where they repaired autos, and Deputy Miller talked about his upcoming hiking trip and how his training program had been affected by the unusually cold weather. Halfway through a pack of cigarettes, Zachary looked up and saw Grace and his wife walking down the hallway towards the exit.

Deputy Miller walked alongside Zachary as they headed towards the women. He was aware of how late it was, and he realized that Grace was probably exhausted. As they got closer, he could not help but notice the transformation. When he first saw Grace, he could tell she was very attractive, even in her state of disarray it was plain to see she was beautiful. Now, she was cleaned up; her hair was combed and her face was clear and bright, but her eyes were troubled. He couldn't pull his gaze away from her.

Deputy Miller was a single man by choice. He did not think it was fair for a woman to live in the shadow of a cop's life. His best friend, Jeremy was his partner. He learned from watching Jeremy and his wife go through the ups and downs of constant worry and fear so he knew that he would be better off alone. Even though loneliness was a bitter pill, he could not think of living any other way.

When they reached the women, Grace gave her daddy a big hug and told him she was grateful that he came to check on her when she was late.

Zachary got angry for a moment. "I only wish to God I that could have caught that bastard. I would have killed him right there!" he said in a loud and forceful voice.

8

"Zachary, calm down! You don't need to get yourself upset again," said Susan.

Deputy Miller understood what Zachary was feeling and he said, "I would probably want to do the same thing if it happened to my daughter. But don't worry we will be doing all we can to find him and put him away."

Deputy Miller looked at his watch and said, "Well, folks, it is getting late and I still needed to go to the crime scene to check in on the investigation. I also have to take care of some paperwork."

Susan gave Deputy Miller a hug and thanked him for his help. He blushed and looked the other way as Grace came towards him and embraced him. This is what he did not want to happen. He just wanted to do his job and go home without getting emotionally involved.

However, Grace was not going to let that happen. He had spent most of the night trying to avoid her, trying to stay focused and in control. Now he was wrapped in the arms of an angel. As she held him, she spoke almost directly into his ear and yet, he never heard a word. He was wrapped in the moment. His heart rate quickened and he shivered as her hair brushed against the side of his face as she released him. He was speechless and the burn in his face told everyone the story in his mind. All he could do was clear his throat and nod his head as he turned and walked off without saying a word.

On his way to his car, he wondered how different his life would be if he had a woman like that to come home to every night—someone to love him and help him over the rough spots that come and go in every cop's life. She would have to be a special lady and those were hard to find.

After checking in at the crime scene, he drove home. When he arrived, his girls were waiting for him. They were ready for their nightly walk and there was no way he was going to let them down. As he approached, they got more and more excited.

"How are my babies doing? Did you have a good day? Did you miss me? I missed you! I am so glad to see you! Let me get my running shoes, girls, and we can go," he said as he hurried into the house.

He lived in a modest little house on the edge of a neighborhood known for its high crime rate, but that never bothered him. He was sure by living where he was, that some of the law-abiding residents would feel safer. The folks he called neighbors were thrilled his two big dogs were around, because they would bark at any strangers walking through the area. Ron was planning to save some money and buy a home in the country where he could hunt and fish more and let the girls have more room to explore and chase a rabbit or squirrel in the woods. He liked walking them; it was a good time to think and plan for the next day or even the next hiking trip. The mountains and rivers were always pulling at his soul to come and explore, and so he spent many hours every week training or practicing for the next adventure.

However, tonight his thoughts would center on a young woman he had just met- a woman who had just been raped and who handled it very well under the circumstances. It crossed his mind how well she stood up to what was ahead of her. The family was in for a rough ride. All Ron could do was catch the guy and hope Grace went on to live a normal life.

Zachary pulled into the driveway and parked the truck. He was exhausted from all the excitement, but sleeping tonight was going to be tough for everyone.

Grace went up to her room and changed for bed. Susan came up after a while to check on her.

"Grace, is there anything you need? Did you take the medication Doctor Cooke gave to you?"

"Yes, Momma," replied Grace. "He said I should sleep pretty well. Momma, why did this have to happen to me? You taught me to respect others and be kind and helpful whenever possible. Did Jesus forget about me?"

"No, Honey! He didn't. He is right here, right now, keeping you safe. Your father and I are here too. Your daddy is probably going to pace all night long. I don't think he could sleep with two of those horse pills the doctor gave you." Susan got a chuckle out of Grace.

"Do you think that man is gone-- or do you think he might try something?"

"I think he is long gone and if he knows what's good for him he'll stay far away from this house, or your father will tear his butt to pieces."

Grace half laughed at the thought of her daddy striking another man. He had a temper and most people who knew him didn't give him a hard time but Grace knew he had a soft side that he hid from others and he wasn't good at showing that side of himself. He grew up during hard times, and his folks were hard on him and his little brother. Growing up poor can leave lasting scars on a man.

Susan was massaging Grace's forehead and whispering Bible passages trying to help her relax and let the medicine take effect. Susan was a deeply religious woman. She held the family together with her spiritual glue. She grew up on the good side of the tracks and was afforded a happy childhood. Never in her wildest dreams did she ever think this kind of horror would visit her doorstep. It wasn't long before Grace was sleeping. Susan left her daughter in the Lord's hands and turned out the light and went to her husband.

Zachary was out in the barn making preparations for a long night of standing guard. He was carrying a loaded shotgun-- and if he could, he was going to use it. When Susan came into the barn, she was startled to see the rifle.

"Zachary what are you doing out here? Why don't you come in and sit with me a while?"

"No, I think I'll stay out here and try to figure this out."

"Zachary, don't you think I need to digest all of this, too? I don't think this is going to be easy for any of us, but I think we need to keep up the appearance of normal for Grace's sake. I think it would frighten her more if she knew you were out here waiting for someone to attack us in the middle of the night."

"Well, maybe you're right. I didn't think about it that way." Zachary looked at his wife like it was the first time all over again and said, "God you're beautiful. What would I do without you? You have always been able to keep me straight."

Zachary put the gun down and took his wife in his arms and squeezed as hard as he could without breaking her petite little body. Susan knew once again she could tame the lion in her man's heart and reveled in the love they shared. As quickly as possible, they closed up the barn and brought the shotgun back into the house. Zachary and Susan stayed up until early morning talking about the next few days and how they were going to change their lives to be more alert and more protective of the ones they loved.

Chapter Two

The next morning Zachary and Grace drove back to the school and the scene of the crime to meet the Assistant District Attorney to find out if they could take her car home. When they arrived, Deputy Miller and two other officers were standing next to a trailer from the county crime scene investigative division. There was yellow crime scene tape attached to orange cones that surrounded the area around Grace's car.

Yellow tape and cones also surrounded a larger perimeter around the vehicles that were parked around Grace's car. They were put there by the first deputy who arrived after they got the call from Zachary about the assault. Inside the smaller circle around Grace's car stood the Assistant District Attorney and five forensic officers. They were checking the ground for any evidence that might still be present. Grace was curious as to what kind of evidence that might be and proceeded to walk up to the trailer to speak to Deputy Miller. "Good morning," said Deputy Miller. "How are you all feeling today?" Zachary wasn't in a good mood. He said a few words under his breath, and Grace chimed in hoping nobody understood what he said. She said, "I feel like a truck has knocked me into a raging bull and then ran me over again. How about you? How are you doing?"

After a few seconds of silence, Deputy Miller said, "Okay, let's go to work," and he motioned towards the door to the trailer and the three went inside.

Inside, the trailer was more of a laboratory on wheels than any kind of a camping trailer Grace had ever seen. There were several refrigerators and freezer units for evidence storage and protection. Deputy Miller pointed to the chairs and motioned for the pair to sit. He was carrying a brief case and he opened it to remove three notepads and some pencils.

He gave Grace and Zachary both a notepad and pencil and asked them to write down anything they could remember about the night before as he asked them questions. He said it was a way for questioning witnesses that usually produced more memory stimulation than just sitting back and fidgeting in a chair.

"Grace, why don't you tell me what happened from the beginning? What took place from the time you exited the school up to when your father found you?

Grace shivered and goose bumps shot down her spine. She really was very sore and although she tried her best to hide her pain, it was obvious to Deputy Miller that this meeting had to move fast so she could get back home and rest.

Grace said, "I came down the sidewalk and started toward my car. I saw two pickup trucks, and there was a rental truck because I remember thinking when I saw it that someone must be moving. Then I tried to get my keys out of my pocket, and the next thing I knew I was being forced to the ground and this heavy, smelly man was on top of me."

It was at that instant, Zachary had heard enough. He stood up and headed for the door without looking back. He closed the door behind him, quickly headed for his truck, and sat in the seat with the door open and his leg hanging out the side. As he lit his cigarette, his mind raced and his stomach turned, and suddenly he vomited violently releasing the rage that had been building inside him. As many as ten grown men saw or heard what had just happened. Not one dared to approach. Zachary pulled a handkerchief from his shirt pocket and wiped the sweat from his brow and slid it down across his face, and then finished his drag on his waiting cigarette.

Grace never knew what happened until she was through with the questioning, and it was then that she saw the mess on the ground next to her father's truck.

"Deputy Miller said he would call the house later to talk to us some

more and fill us in on what is going on with the investigation.   He said we could take the car home soon.   Since it was locked there should not be any evidence in it, and there doesn't appear to be any finger prints on it."
Grace hesitated then continued, "Daddy, I don't want to drive it.   Do you think you could get it home for me later?"

"Sure.   I will come by with one of the guys from the shop later this afternoon.   Don't you worry about it honey."

Later that morning, Grace and Susan were in the kitchen preparing lunch.   Grace was usually at school during this time of the day, and Susan was normally at her office job keeping the books for Mr. Forrester who owned a fabric shop in town.   Zachary decided he would be better off at the garage.   He didn't need to be there, but it would keep him busy, and he needed to focus his energy on something constructive.   Alex was at school—he was being held to his normal daily routine.

"Momma, while I was talking to Deputy Miller, he said that there was another girl attacked in Hawfields last month, and there was a rental truck parked near the place where she was attacked.   He thinks there may be a connection because the truck I saw last night was gone when the deputy arrived to secure the crime scene.   He said the guy probably worked alone, and he thinks it is possible that he runs to a predetermined spot to hide and watch his victim run off.   Then he hops in the truck to make his get-away. If you think about it, it is easy to steal a rental truck and drive it around because of the similarities.   The police would have to stop almost every one because the guy may be replacing his license plates with other trucks as he goes.   He's essentially able to run free, but according to Deputy Miller, that is just one of the many working theories they have, but other possibilities are being investigated."

Grace sat looking out the window for a few minutes.   "Momma, I don't want to go anywhere for a while, and I want to take a break from school.   I'm not sure I even want to go back."

Susan's eyes filled with tears.   She was afraid that this would happen, and still she couldn't decide if it was for the best or not.

"The story came out in the newspaper this morning, and ever since then the phone has rung over twenty times, mostly family and friends, but the local news has been hounding for an interview.   I don't think anyone would blame you for taking some time off honey," said Susan, "but I think you should at least try to keep up with your classes.   You may feel differently in a couple weeks after you had a good rest.   Let's take it one day at a time and let the Lord show us the way, all right?"   Grace got up and hugged her mom for a long time then went to her room for the rest of the day.

Deputy Miller called around dinnertime and Susan explained that the family was not up for a visit and that he should call Zachary at the shop to inform him of any new developments.

Weeks went by and nothing changed.   The police were still searching for leads and the whole family was still numb and jumpy.   The slightest abnormal sounds in the night would send goose bumps over Grace's body. At least once a week she could hear her daddy go outside to pacify her momma to be sure some obscure sound from the garage was just a cat knocking over a can and not somebody intending to do them harm.

Her days were filled with hours of silence—she kept the radio and TV off, left the bathroom light on, and made sure the doors were locked at least three times a day.   When Alex came home from school, she would watch TV, feeling a little safer with even him around.   At night, the family would huddle close together in the living room and watch TV until bedtime.   Even though the nights began to feel a little more normal, there was still a cautious measure of uncertainty. Until the menace that haunted her dreams was caught, she could never get on with her life.   Grace's depression deepened as the days rolled by, her own self-pity was slowly consuming her, until a tragedy that more than rivaled her own happened on a rainy March morning just a few miles out of town.

Chapter Three

Susan's baby brother was just a few years older than Grace; he was wild and reckless and lived life on the edge.   Jack was always in trouble with the law, racing cars on the streets, and fighting in the bars.   But he had a good heart, and you could always count on him for a favor.   He worked for a logging company, and his job was delivering fully loaded trucks to local sawmills.

On this particular day, the winds were gusting and rain showers came and went. Some with such blinding intensity that the traffic slowed to a crawl and even the most experienced drivers pulled over to stop under a bridge or overpass.   Jack was driving along a two lane back road headed for Martin's Saw Mill in Liberty to the south, thinking if he didn't make up some time, his girlfriend Brenda would surely be eating her lunch alone. He may have been going too fast.   As he headed down a long hill that was fairly straight for a few miles, he could see the lights at the railroad crossing starting to flash.   As he pushed his foot down on the brake pedal, it went straight to the floor!   The truck wasn't going to stop and Jack knew it. He tried to jam the transmission into a lower gear to slow down as much as possible.

Jack slammed into the fifth car of a twenty-two-car train.   Although the train didn't jump the tracks, it caught the front end of the truck at impact and tossed it off to the side as the trailer full of logs flipped. Luckily, it scattered toward the rear of the train and never got close to hitting any of the other waiting cars.   In the cab, anything not bolted down flew past Jack's head.   When the truck came in at impact, Jack cut the wheel hard to try to get the front end of the cab turned in the direction the train was traveling hoping it would help him bounce off and out of the way of the trailer carrying the logs.   The closer he got, the faster his mind's eye flashed the faces of the people in his life.

Jack's body twisted in the outdated seatbelt system, and his head smashed against the door, knocking him out cold.   Within seconds it was over, and it was difficult to tell that the mangled metal, plastic, wires and glass were once a truck.   The gas from the carburetor ran onto the manifold, and in a flash a small fire ignited.   The gas continued to leak and the fire grew, consuming anything in its path.   People were pulling up in cars from behind and running to the scene.

"Who has a fire extinguisher?   Does anyone have a fire extinguisher?" someone called out, but no one answered.

Some men tried to beat the fire out with blankets and the shirts off their backs.   They couldn't see Jack through the smoke, but those determined folks knew someone had to be in the truck, and they were hell bent to get them out.   The smoke and flames were too much for anyone. The onlookers stepped back further and further expecting the cab to explode.

All at once the skies opened up with a mighty flash of lighting striking the ground across the tracks.   As the roll of thunder grew louder, the rain came down in buckets soaking anyone or anything not covered or protected including an aspiring gasoline fire in a race for its own survival. Like a gift from heaven, the downpour lasted long enough for a few brave men to pull Jack to safety.   As they carried him away from the smoldering wreck, the deluge of rain that slowed the flames from consuming the lifeless body inside subsided, and the fire gained new life, intensifying and burning the truck in an inferno of flames.   Only minutes elapsed from impact to the instant Jack was safe.   Several bystanders held blankets over his bloodied and broken body.   Someone from the crowd announced an ambulance was on the way.

At three o'clock that afternoon, Susan called Grace and told her what had happened.   She suggested Grace and Alex drive to the hospital to meet them and the rest of the family.   Grace had not been out much, and her car had not been driven since it was parked nearly a month earlier; but Jack was one of her favorite people in the world and nothing was going to keep her from getting to him.

18

"Alex, Uncle Jack has been in a wreck!" Grace yelled after hanging up the phone. "Momma wants us to meet her at the hospital right away. It's serious! They don't know if he is going to make it!"

Alex was a lot like Jack and he idolized him. He raced down the stairs to Grace's waiting car. In no time at all they were both headed to Alamance Regional Medical Center. Alex's heart raced; he was scared and nervous and rattling off questions to which Grace had no answers.

"What did Momma say happened?" asked Alex.

"She told me that Uncle Jack was in a wreck. He was in bad shape, and they were waiting for him to come out of surgery. That's it, I swear! I don't know what else to tell you. Momma said she didn't have time to explain. She had to make other phone calls and then go back to the waiting room where Daddy was with Brenda. Oh, poor Brenda! She must be a nervous wreck!" said Grace.

"I bet he will be alright. Yeah, I bet he'll be just fine," Alex said in the most believable way he could. However, inside, he was still afraid. She turned and looked at him and said, "Of course he will! Now just relax and listen to the radio."

"Yeah, that's a good idea. Listen to the radio." Alex turned the car stereo on and began to channel surf. He came across his favorite country station in time to hear Willie Nelson's latest hit song. He was beginning to settle down when the news came on reporting that a train hit a logging truck and right away it was clear to them both that Jack was in rough shape. Alex kept saying, "Oh my God! Oh my God! I hope he is okay."

At the hospital, Zachary and Susan sat with Brenda as she wept. She had not seen Jack, but the doctors and nurses didn't give him much hope, and told them to be prepared for the worst.

Some friends and family began to arrive and the little waiting area began to fill very quickly. Soon folks were reminiscing and telling stories and tales about Jack and his adventures. Grace and Alex greeted family and friends as they made their way to Brenda.   They found Zachary and Susan and settled in to wait out the night—to pray for Jack to survive the surgery and make it through the night.   The last words from a passing nurse gave everybody hope when she said, "So far so good."

Grace found her first public appearance to be very unnerving.   Two hours had passed since she arrived, and she was feeling like a guppy in a fish bowl.   She could feel the looks burn through her.   She was trying to guess what these people were thinking of her.   She felt as if some of them were trying to hide their eyes—perhaps to hide their own self-doubt for how they might handle the horror of Grace's ordeal.   To her, it was more of a guilty feeling for a crime she did not commit.   No one could understand the realities of her inner turmoil unless they had been raped, too.   She had to get some fresh air.   She needed to be out of the light and go into the shadows where she could hide.

"Momma will you walk with me?" she asked, but Susan didn't seem to get the meaning in her tone.

Grace looked at her daddy and he saw in her eyes what her momma didn't hear in her voice.   Zachary said, "I need a cigarette.   Would you mind going with me to the truck?   You can get some fresh air?"

It was the escape that Grace was hoping for.   They slipped out of the waiting room unnoticed and made their way to the parking lot.   Zachary didn't speak until they were outside.

"What's wrong, baby girl?   What's bothering you," he asked?

"Oh Daddy, I just felt weird with all those people in there, looking at me and whispering to each other.   I just wanted to get away.   Didn't you see Aunt Martha?   She's the worst one.   Remember when she came to visit after it happened?   She acted like I was a used rag.   She made me feel so cheap and dirty; suggesting I move out of town and make a new start where people didn't know what had happened, like it was my own fault—as if I asked for it and got caught.   She acted like I was an embarrassment to the family.   I shouldn't have to be the one to pay, and yet I am.   Every day I pay; I am hiding away consumed with fear and that…that monster is free!"   Grace's face was red with embarrassment; she was so angry at the world she had to let it out.

"Grace, you can't stay inside the house forever.   There will be a time when this will pass.   Maybe you should think outside the box for now.   If Jack pulls through the surgery, he's going to need a lot of support."

Grace replied, "So you want me to help Jack and Brenda?"

"Yes, I think it would be a blessing for them to have you around to help out, and it would keep you from feeling like you're going crazy.   You can't stay cooped up in your room forever."

Grace knew her daddy was right.   She had been feeling very sorry for herself, and that was not the Grace she and her daddy knew.   She got the message.

"Oh, daddy, I hope Jack is alright.   I am going to do it!   I am going to get off my butt and start living again!"   Grace felt better about herself and her problems seemed to be so much smaller than they were upstairs in the crowded waiting area.   "Daddy, I am going back up to sit with Brenda and Momma."   Grace gave her daddy a big hug; "I love you and Momma so much; I would die if anything happened to you!"

"I think we'll be safe tonight.   One day at a time," said Zachary and then he told Grace to tell her Mom he would be up shortly.

When Grace arrived back to the waiting area, there was a lot of commotion and people were standing in line at the phone booth ten deep. Susan and Brenda were hugging and crying.   People were gathered around with tissues, and tears were falling in even the toughest of old men.

"What happened?" called Grace in full stride towards her Mom.

"Jack's surgery is over and the doctor just left. He made it!   He said Jack was going to live, but they're uncertain if he will ever walk again. We're all so grateful he is alive.   We need to continue to pray for the swelling to go down so he'll be able to walk into his home on his own two feet!"

"Oh, Momma, that's wonderful news! When can we see him?"

"I don't know. They didn't say anything about visitation. I will ask the nurse the next time she comes out."

"Daddy said he would be right up, but I've just got to run down and tell him right now!"

Grace was off running past Alex, who was standing with some folks who were asking him to recall the football game at the high school last Friday night. Alex was doing his best to make it sound exciting, but he really didn't watch much of the game; since he was more interested in the girls that went to the games. "Hey, there goes my sister! I better see where she's off to," he said as he took off after Grace.

Zachary was waiting for the elevator to come down from the third floor. He was dreading what he may learn when he got back up to the waiting area. When the doors slid open, there was Grace standing alone with an ear-to-ear smile on her face.

Zachary could tell good news just found him. She jumped onto her Dad wrapping her arms around his neck, nearly knocking him to the ground. "You damn near knocked me on my ass you nut!" said Zachary gasping for air. "Jack's out of surgery, and they said he's going to be alright, except he might not be able to walk. But it's too soon to know for sure." The elevator door closed without them. Zachary looked at Grace and said, "I think I have been here before."

Grace laughed with him. They both needed a good laugh. It was good medicine. They stood there watching the elevator light climb to the top and back down again. When it opened, it was full and people piled out; some stopping to talk to Zachary and Grace saying goodnight and giving each other celebratory hugs. Among them was Alex. He joined in the departing gestures and the elevator closed. Zachary and Grace laughed again and told Alex what had just happened as they waited for it to come down again hoping Susan was on the next load, but she wasn't. So the three of them jumped in and rode to the third floor.

When the door opened Susan was there waiting on the other side for a ride down, "Hurry and get in!" yelled Alex. Susan stepped into the elevator and Alex and Grace laughed.

Susan said, "You kids are crazy. What's going on?"

Zachary said, "Never mind for now. What's going on with Jack? Grace said he might be paralyzed?"

"They don't know that for sure. He needs to rest and let the swelling go down, but he did break his neck—and that's never a good thing. We all just have to pray and wait to see."

"When can we see him?" asked Grace.

"Hopefully we can see him in a few days, but he's in a coma. They don't think he'll be waking up for days because of the drugs they are giving him. He has a risk of infection and he must stay still so his neck can heal properly. It's all in God's hands now."

Chapter Four

Three days later Grace entered the hospital to visit Jack.   On the way to the elevator, her eye caught Deputy Ron Miller standing at a pay phone in the lobby.   "Ugh," she gasped, "Oh my God, I don't want him to see me," she said to herself and she swiftly turned into the gift shop which actually had glass windows to the main hall.   She pretended to shop for little clay figurines in the window, but she was actually trying to get a look at Deputy Miller.

"Can I help you, Miss?" said the sales clerk almost startling Grace.

"Oh!   Yes, sure." stammered Grace as she turned her eyes from Ron and looked at the cashier.   I am looking for something to cheer up my uncle.   He was in a terrible wreck, and I want to give him something different.   What do you have that's not too expensive, but will bring a smile to his face?"

"Ummm," said the lady, "I think you might want to try some of the get well cards over on the back wall."   As Grace turned to look, the lady said, "There are a lot of cute cards that are quite affordable."

Grace was amazed at the variety and finding one to suit Jack was not a problem.   After scanning through several cards, she settled on one. She handed it to the cashier.   The lady put it in a bag and asked for a dollar and seventy-five cents. Grace said, "That is a cheap way to give someone a laugh!"

Grace hadn't noticed Ron wasn't at the phone when she left the gift shop and headed towards the elevators.   As she rounded the corner, there, standing at the door to the elevator, was Ron.   'Oh no, he sees me. I guess I can't avoid him this time,' she thought to herself.

As she approached, she couldn't help but notice how handsome he was. It had been a while since they had met at the school parking lot, and she was pretty off balanced then. Much of what happened seemed a blur now.

Ron couldn't believe his eyes when Grace came around that corner. She was dressed simply and yet in the most sophisticated way. She carried herself like a proud princess. Grace had put her hair up and tied it with a red ribbon. She wore earrings with little eight balls because she knew Jack liked to play pool at the clubs. The weather was warming up, and spring was surely in the air, so Grace wore her favorite turtle neck sweater, snug fitting jeans and machine washed white tennis shoes.

Ron was on duty, but his lonely hunger for love and his strong desire for Grace were hard to keep in check. He wished he had never met her. How could he ever think he would forget her? "Hello, Miss Grace, how's it going this bright and beautiful morning?" asked Ron.

"Fine, thank you. It is nice out. I love the warm weather. It's nice to get out and smell the fresh spring air," she replied. She had a side to her only her best friends and some past boyfriends got the privilege to see. Therefore, she just had to ask, "Every time I see you, you're wearing a uniform. Do you ever take it off?" Ron looked at her puzzled.

Grace blushed and quickly followed, "I mean do you ever take a day off?"

"Oh…so you're a wise-cracker?" asked Ron. She laughed out loud covering her mouth to keep from attracting attention from the passersby in the hall.

"I can be," she replied. The door opened, "Ladies before gentleman," said Ron and he bowed allowing her to enter the elevator before him.

"Why thank you, kind sir," she said in her best southern drawl. She turned and grabbed onto the handrail. Ron stepped in and they both stared forward as the elevator door closed.   He asked her which floor she would like and she replied, "I'm going up to the third floor."   He pressed three and up they went.

The door opened and Grace stepped out.   She turned to say good-bye to Ron and he walked right into her.   She didn't know, but he too was getting off at the third floor.

"I'm sorry.   Are you okay?" he asked, "I didn't think you were going to stop like that!"

Her nose was stinging; and she said from under the cover of her hand over her nose, "I didn't know you were getting off on this floor, too.   It's alright.   I'll be okay.   After all, look where we are.   What better place to get a bloody nose!"   She pulled a tissue from her purse, held it on her nose, and started walking.   "I guess I'll see you around," she said.

Ron replied, "I think I'm going this way, too.   So I will see you around now."   They walked down the hall side-by-side and step-by-step until Grace arrived at Jack's room.   She turned to Ron and said, "It was nice talking to you again, and I hope you have a good day. I'm visiting my uncle.   He was in a wreck a few days ago."

Ron just looked at her and said, "Miss Grace, I believe I should go first and make sure the coast is clear," and Ron stepped in front of her and walked by her into Jack's room.   Now Grace had that puzzled look, so she followed him into the room.   "Hello," he whispered, "I'm Deputy Miller. Is he awake?"

Grace had not yet seen Jack.   She was told what to expect, but she was not prepared for what he looked like in person.   Upon a closer look, she was horrified by the magnitude of his injuries.   His head was surrounded by a halo with four long steel rods sliding into his head and screwed into his skull to keep his head still.   His face was so swollen and bruised it was nearly impossible to recognize him unless you looked into his eyes, and the fire that burned inside him was the only thing that looked familiar.   He was burned on his left shoulder; the bandages were being

26

changed every hour to keep the wound cool and moist.   The halo was connected to a body cast that went all the way to his kneecaps.   She could see his legs and feet were covered in varied degrees of bruises and scrapes. He was strapped to the bed for his own safety.   A constant morphine drip was his only comfort, if there was one.   She couldn't help but tear up and went for the tissue box on the nightstand next to his bed.   A nurse was sitting in the corner below a TV mounted on the wall.   Grace had not noticed her when she first entered Jack's room.   "Don't worry darlin, he doesn't feel a thing.   We try to make sure of that.   The only thing is he may not remember you being here, but he is able to answer you if you talk slowly and clearly."

Grace leaned over his face and asked, "Can you hear me, Jack?   It's Grace."

He whispered a weak "Yeah."

"Do you need anything?"   After a long pause, "Bike," he whispered, and she started to laugh and cry at the same time.

The nurse asked, "What did he say?"

"He said he wanted his bike.   He has a Harley Davidson Motorcycle that he's been cleaning up and detailing in the living room of the house he rents.   I was there at Christmas and he was telling me that he couldn't wait to drive it to Myrtle Beach for bike week in June."   The tears came more than the laughter as she realized he might never ride a motorcycle again. Ron stood back and never said a word.   He was speechless.   He wanted to comfort her, to take her in his arms.   Instead, he backed out of the room and headed down the hall to the elevator.   Jack's statement will have to come later. Right now, he needed to get back to work.

Ron filled the rest of his day with deep thought.   It was hard to keep his mind on the job.   His view of life had once again been reshaped by life itself.   The profound effects he was sure would be revealed.   Driving home he thought about his life and all that he thought was important the day before.   Yesterday, on his ride home from work, he was excited about a short hiking trip he was taking Sunday morning before church. His heart started to race. He said to himself, 'Thank you Lord for the blessings you have given me; surely I would be miserable without my legs. I don't know how I would make it. God help that man.' As he pulled into his driveway, he resolved to put the bad feelings away until tomorrow.

Chapter Five

Magic and Boo were always the best medicine when things got too bad at work.   He knew he would be coming home to his two true unconditional loves--the best kind.   These two dogs were never tired of being loved.

"Hey girls!   How are we doing today?   You want to go for a walk, huh?   You ready to go?   Let me get changed and we're off."

Ron let the dogs follow him in the house.   They watched with excitement as he changed into his sweat pants and running shoes.   Magic and Boo were very well trained and knew where they could and couldn't go when inside the house.   They stood at his bedroom door looking in, and both of them started talking in that dog language only a dog can understand.   These two sisters were mixed breeds and had a wolf for a grandpa.   They gave Ron a rumbling groan that he had learned to mimic and he talked back to them.   They loved to hear him.   He could get them revved up in minutes until they started barking and banging into each other. "Alright!   Easy!   Easy!" said Ron, "we'll be out of here in a second. Let's get your leashes."

Boo is always too excited to stay still, so she always takes the longest to get ready every night.   Magic is the sweetest dog hybrid you would ever wish to have.   She looks like a black wolf with some dog features.   She's got magic eyes.   They seem to glow when she stares you down.   She may be the tougher of the two, but Boo is most certainly the boss—the alpha female.

They pulled Ron down the driveway and onto the road.   He was walking along almost in a trance.   They had walked this mile loop so many times he didn't need to pay close attention, so it was the best time for serious thinking.   He thought about his dad, Reno.   'I think I will call him tonight,' he thought, 'see what he's up to. I haven't seen him in a couple weeks.   Maybe he'll have a good joke for me.'   Ron walked the four miles and turned the dogs up the driveway before they had him walk another.   They could go all night, but he had other things to tend to.

Later that night he called his dad, "Hey man, what's up?" asked Ron.

"Hey what's up with you?" asked Reno, and they both chuckled.   It was the same greeting they had given each other for years.

"Hey, you got a minute to talk?" asked Ron.

"Sure," said Reno. "What do you got?"

"I have been going through these changes." He was having trouble finding the words to explain his dilemma. "I've been thinking," and he groaned out load.

"What's bothering you kid?" asked Reno.

"Well, I have been thinking about this girl I met," he said.

Reno said, "Now I see, and you want me to call her for you?"

"No.   No, I don't want you to call her for me.   She is part of an on-going investigation, and I was the lucky guy on duty that night.   Even though I am not assigned to the case, I still think it is improper to get involved."

"What do you mean by involved?"

"You know, like maybe go for walks and coffee and stuff like that."

"So what you're trying to say is you want to get in her pants!"

"Thanks Dad.   I can always count on you to set the record straight!"

"Hey!   No problem kid.   That's what I'm here for."

"Yeah, thanks."

Chapter Six

Grace was exhausted when she plopped herself on the living room sofa that night. Susan was already sitting, reading a fashion magazine. The TV was turned down low, but you could still hear it, only a lamp on the end table next to the sofa was on for light. Susan had positioned her pillow on the sofa to allow her the full benefit of its glow to read in blissful comfort. Without looking up from her page, Susan asked what she thought when she first saw Jack this morning.

"It was awful," said Grace. "I can't believe he lived. Momma, I never thought anything like that was possible. He is so swollen that you can't even recognize him! Oh, I can't even think about it now. I'm just too tired. He is so lucky he's alive, but what a price to pay."

Susan said, "You know the Lord has a plan and we are all just a little piece of the big puzzle. I am sure Jack will heal, and maybe in time he'll look more like himself; and who knows, he may even be able to walk once all the swelling is gone."

"I hope so," said Grace "but I think his Harley will have to be sold to help pay his rent. I don't know what he is going to do when he gets home. Momma, where will he stay? He can't pay his bills, and you know his benefits from work won't be here for months. You know how that works!"

"Don't you worry about a thing. Your daddy's out there right now with Alex. They're cleaning the place and locking everything up. Daddy paid for the next three months' rent on the house, so he doesn't have to worry for a while; and if he mentions it, you tell him he can pay us back when he gets back to work."

"What a relief! He'll be so relieved when I tell him! Brenda and I were speaking, and she was telling me that they were thinking of renting a storage unit for all his stuff. I know she will appreciate it. This will give them more time to plan for his rehab when he is able to leave the hospital. Momma, I saw Deputy Miller at the hospital. I think I may have embarrassed him. When I saw Jack, I just fell apart. I was so shocked. Anyway, by the time I wiped my eyes, he was gone. Oh, Momma, I must have been a mess! I was blowing my nose and just going through that tissue box; I must have been a sight! He's pretty handsome, and he doesn't wear a wedding ring, so I'm pretty sure he's not married. I wonder if he has a girlfriend."

"You're such a crazy girl," said Susan, "You haven't changed a bit. You've been talking about boys since you were twelve, and you still got that wild look in your eye when you do it now!" The two women laughed more like sisters than mother and daughter. Grace thought, 'After that night, I wasn't sure I'd ever be attracted to a man ever again. It's good to know I can feel something again!'

"Well, I'm going to go get ready for bed," said Grace and she leaned on her momma crushing her magazine in between them. She squeezed Susan and said, "Good night, I love you!" and Susan let out her breath and said, "I love you, too."

Susan lay back on her pillow and smiled, glad that some things were returning to normal. Grace had been on track to becoming a promising scientist until that night. Now, she didn't know what the future held for her daughter, but she was certain Grace was growing stronger and would be ready to face it.

Chapter Seven

Six weeks had passed since Jack's wreck.   Spring was in full bloom. Grace had several meetings with the District Attorney and his assistant, but there had been no new leads until one Tuesday night.   Grace and the family were having dinner and watching the news, when a story broke about an attempted rape in Raleigh.   The man caught was believed to be driving a rented U-Haul truck.   The whole family stared at the TV in silence.   Grace was hoping this day wouldn't come as much as she knew it would.   She looked at her daddy and said, "You see this kind of stuff on the news all the time, but it's so different when you know it's about you."

"Well, I guess if this is the guy, then we will probably be hearing from the District Attorney anytime now," said Zachary.

"I hope it's him," said Susan, "that guy will kill someone, if they don't put him away soon."

"I hope I don't have to meet the D.A. tomorrow.   I am going to see Jack to help him with his exercises," said Grace. "He needs to keep trying. I'm going to make sure he does."

"We're very proud of you, Grace.   Brenda said she would be helpless without you," said Susan.

"If Jack never walks, it won't be for lack of trying," said Zachary.

A few weeks later Grace was in Raleigh at the County House of Corrections for a lineup.   She was to pick out her rapist from a group of similarly looking men.   Grace didn't want to do it for fear they could see her from the other side of the window.   Susan and Grace stood huddled together in the middle of a dimly lit room.   Grace peered out towards the men, hoping she was hidden from their view.   Her eyes scanned the first man, and she looked him up and down trying to imagine how her rapist might look now.   She looked hurriedly over the rest, back-and-forth several times, until she saw something familiar—and it was him.   Her rapist was number five!   She was sure of it; he was the one!   Her heart was racing.   She couldn't get it out, and she was breathing heavy and started to choke.   She was hyperventilating.   She wanted so desperately to get it out, and tell everyone that was him—that he was the man that raped her.   However, she was helpless.   Just like that night in the frozen cold of winter, when he knocked her over, held a knife to her throat, and threatened her life if she ever told.   She fell back into a large cushioned leather chair and felt a paper bag come over her face.   She fought back as best she could in her numb and dizzy state of mind.   It took a few moments for her to catch her breath and collect her thoughts.   "That's the guy," she said calmly, pointing to number five.

The D.A. asked, "Which one is it, Grace?"

"Him, number five," she said.

"Are you sure, Grace?" asked the D.A.

Grace said, "Yes, that's him. I'm sure."

"That's the guy we picked up in Raleigh.   We will charge him with aggravated assault, and rape and the judge will set bail in the morning, but he will not be able to afford it.   I will see to that.   Grace, we are going to need you to come in sometime next week so we can start preparing you for the trial.   I think we have enough evidence to put this guy away for a long time with your help and the help of the girl he attacked in Raleigh.   We should have plenty of eyewitness testimony to back it all up.   Okay Grace, Mrs. Fields, let me show you out."

The D.A. walked Grace and Susan to the front desk by the entrance, and he thanked them both for their patience promising to do everything in his power to get a conviction and a long jail sentence.

In less than three months, Jack was home learning to live his life in a wheel chair. Grace was using his accident to keep herself so busy she wouldn't have to think of her own life. Roger Baker was the name of the man who raped her. His trial was due to start within a week. She was afraid to come face-to-face with him. Hanging around Jack was comforting to her. He was the only one she could talk to when it was hardest to be strong—when giving up was on her mind. It was Jack who kept her going. Grace never told Susan or Zachary how close she came to killing herself, but Jack knew. They spent many hours talking each other out of giving up. Jack had his days when self-pity was stronger than his desire to go on living. Grace pushed Jack whenever he thought he could do no more, she forced him to the next level. Brenda said he would not have made it out of the hospital so soon were it not for Grace.

Chapter Eight

The temperature was rising.   It was late in the spring, and schools everywhere were winding down to the end of the year finals.   Grace always loved this time of the year; it was perfect weather for hikes in the woods.   The summers were too warm and buggy.   You could catch a face full of spider webs and bees everywhere you went.   When Grace was a little girl, she had a bad allergic reaction to a bee sting.   She stepped on a nest while playing in the fields behind the barn at her grandma's house in Snow Camp.

Grace loved going to the farm, she always had a wonderful time. There was always something to do.   Her Grandpa was a handy, crafty ole farmer. He came up the hard way, back in the Depression.   It was certainly an era when you learned how to do it or make it yourself, or you went without.   Grace will never forget that day when she was stung.   She ended up nearly comatose before they finally got her to the emergency room at the old hospital.   Nobody knew what had happened, and Grace's throat had become so swollen she couldn't speak.   She was scared and so was everyone else.   Grandma Palmer recognized the symptoms and located the stinger on her foot. That had happened a long time ago, but the memory was as fresh as if it had happened yesterday.

Today she was going to Cedar Rock Park to spend the day looking for spring flowers and soaking in the sunshine.   Nothing was going to bother her today.   The court was still picking a jury and she was not needed for that.   Jack was spending the day with Brenda who was shuttling him around town to different appointments.   The day was all hers.   The sun and warm breeze were all she needed.   Parking her car, she noticed several other vehicles in the lot besides her.   She scrutinized each one, and tried to remember what each one was and even the plate numbers.   She was determined to memorize each one.   Walking past a red jeep, she noticed an emblem on the back bumper; it said 'Support Your Local Sheriff Department'. 'Um, she thought, I wonder if there's a cop in there.' The thought of a cop walking the same trails as she made her feel somewhat safer, but she still wasn't going to trust anyone, even if they were in uniform. After a few minutes to tighten her shoes and get her pack straightened out, she was off.

'My God, what a gorgeous day,' she thought. 'I can't wait until this crap is over and I can just get on with my life.' She spent the morning exploring the trails, checking out the springtime surprises. A little green frog hopped onto the path in front of her and she tried to catch it; instead falling to the ground and laughing aloud like a child blowing out her birthday candles at her first real party. Butterflies were everywhere, in all colors and sizes searching for nectar in the sea of yellow, blue and red wild flowers. She tried to be quiet for the most part, but she knew that there were other hikers in the park, so the chances of seeing deer were slim, but that did not deter her from keeping an eye in the woods and listening close when she came to areas where she had seen deer before. She was hoping for a glimpse at this year's crop of fawns.

For lunch, she brought a ham sandwich with mayonnaise, mustard, lettuce, tomato and cheese with a side of potatoes chips, cookies, an apple and large bottle of water that she had already drank half of by lunch time. Munching on the delicious sandwich, she lay back in the grass and stared up into the sky dreaming of a day when she'd be a wife and mom with a career living a 'normal' life. The clouds were large and fluffy white. Every couple of minutes the sun would pop out from behind the clouds and momentarily blind her. She shielded her eyes with her hand as she waited for the next one to move in its way. 'I wish this day would last forever,' she thought.

After cleaning up from lunch, she headed back off down the trail. Cedar Rock Park has a vast maze of trails in the core of the park, but a trail designated specifically for horses and adventure hikers meandered in a large circle on the outer edges of the park. It was her favorite trail. It was less traveled, and it took most of the day if you took your time. It had rained a few days ago so some of the horse's footprints were still full of rainwater. She imagined she was discovering dinosaur fossil footprints, and marveled how such an event could actually occur.

A few hours after lunch, she came upon acres of wild flowers in a field, in the middle of the woods. She was so proud of herself, selfishly thinking she was the only one who would ever be so lucky to see this field in full bloom. Then she heard a noise a few feet in front of her and she froze. Was it a snake? She had no idea what was stirring in the grass and flowers in front of her. She strained her neck trying to see what was in there. "Oh!" she gasped. "Oh My Gosh!" she said, "what a precious little darling." She moved one-step closer and there, lying in the grass, was a terrified little fawn full of spots and incredibly beautiful. She could see its little heart was racing in its chest. She watched in amazement for a few moments then slowly backed up trying not to cause the poor thing to flee possibly injuring itself. She couldn't get over watching the little deer blinking its eyes, but not moving in the slightest bit. She was ready to go home now. 'I don't know how this day could get any better!' she thought. She started down the trail, and thought about her mom and how nice it would be to surprise her with a vase full of daisies. She decided to pick a few to bring home. She was aware that she was taking her chances messing around with flowers.

She was hoping it was too early to worry about bees, since the flowers had only been out for a few days and she hadn't seen any bees all day. She gathered up a fairly good armful and headed for home. She had about a quarter of the trip left when she felt a sharp pinch on her arm. The sudden burn and stinging pain registered immediately in her brain. She threw the flowers and looked at her forearm. A whelt was developing in front of her eyes and she started to panic. "What am I going to do?" What the hell bit me?" she cried out loud. She kicked the pile of daises on the ground, and then she saw what it was. A hornet must have been hiding in the mass of flowers when she was picking them, and he took his anger out on Grace by stinging her.

Grace knew she was in trouble; even if she made it to her car how would she get to the hospital?   She started running as fast as she could. She didn't know she was circulating the venom through her blood stream faster than if she walked out relaxed and calm.   She lost her breath after a few hundred yards.   She could feel her arm burning like fire; her chest grew tight and her throat was dry and getting tighter.   She was in trouble. She heard something in the distance; she knew she was too far from the parking lot, so it must be someone coming down the trail.   She tried to call out as loud as she could.   Sweat poured down her face; she was getting weak.   The pain in her chest increased.   She dropped to her knees and tried to yell again, but nothing came out, just a squeaky whistle.   She leaned against a tree and rolled over to lay back.   She was having trouble focusing and holding up her head.   Suddenly, out of nowhere, she thought she saw a dog.   She didn't even have the strength to raise her arms when the dog started to lick her face, and then there was another one.   Both dogs were licking her cheeks.   She felt like she was in a dream, and then she passed out and slid off the tree trunk face down into the leaves.

The dogs started to bark at her, but she could barely hear them.   Ron was rounding a knoll when he heard the dogs barking.   From a distance, he could see Magic and Boo harassing something on the ground in front of them.   He picked up the pace to get there before they hurt some little deer or destroyed a rabbit's nest.   They were good at finding game in the woods, and they liked nothing more than chasing squirrels and rabbits. "What the heck?" said Ron, and he ran to what he now knew was a body on the ground.   "Get back girls," he yelled to the dogs, "get out of the way."   They were just as worried as he was.   Ron got down to his knees and carefully leaned in and put his head on Grace's back and listening for a heartbeat.   She was wheezing heavily but her heart was still beating.

He didn't recognize the girl he was saving.   Her face had swollen and she was hot and sweaty.   Ron had Red Cross and CPR training on a regular basis as part of his law enforcement duties.   He began to assess her injuries.   He didn't see any blood around her head or neck, but she was straining to breathe, so he opened her mouth and looked inside, running his fingers inside her mouth.   His mind was working fast.   What is happening to this girl?   Then he thought of an overdose of drugs.   He checked out her arms and saw a large swollen area on her forearm. He looked at it closely, and it hit him like a rock. This girl was going into anaphylactic shock! He went for his pack and slung it off his back and fumbled while he tried to unfasten the old broken zipper to get at his first aid kit. He pulled out his last EPI pen, left over from last year, and said, "Please God let me save this girl's life." He injected the serum into her arm. He took his sweater from his pack, and putting it on the ground, he propped up her head with his pack.

He picked up her backpack to look for some identification; all he found was a set of keys with a charm that read Grace. Ron's heart sank; he got up close to her and moved her hair back and looked through the redness of her puffy face. He knew it was his Grace who was counting on him to keep her alive.

Ron knew he couldn't get her out alone. He was going to have to leave her here, and go call for help. It was his only chance to save her. He tried to get her to drink some water, but she was still unconscious. He picked up the sweater and wrapped her in it, trying to keep her warm. Ron wasn't sure if leaving was the best thing. What if she didn't make it and he wasn't there with her? He leaned in over her face; he stared at her and begged, "Please Grace, don't give up. I need you." He softly whispered a kiss on her lips, and he knew he could never kiss another.

He got up and said, "Stay!" to Magic and Boo. He turned around and ran as fast as he could—as fast as he ever had—until he reached the pay phone at the restroom kiosk. He called for a rescue squad with the capability of a woodland extraction. Grace would have to be carried out by specially trained Emergency Medical Technicians. He explained in great detail the trail they were on, and how far down they would have to travel. He didn't stay on the phone long. In just moments he was running back to Grace.

Grace was awake when he returned. Magic and Boo were lying on each side of her with their heads on her lap. She was spoiling them both. He was huffing and puffing when he approached. "Are you all right? Do you want something to drink?" he asked.

"Yes, please," answered Grace.   "How did you find me?" she asked.

Still out of breath, he managed to explain how he and the girls came upon her, and how he had given her a shot from an EPI pen he was not sure would be any good.

"Apparently it was good enough," she said "but I am still a little woozy. I bet I would puke if I were to stand up!"

Ron said "Oh no, don't even think about it.   There is a rescue team from the fire department on the way.   These are friends of mine.   They will take good care of you, so just relax and take it easy."

She looked at him and said, "You're kidding!   You mean to tell me I am going to be carried out of here?   I don't think so!"   She tried to stand up, almost knocking her head into a low tree limb.   He grabbed her by the arm and said, "Whoa there, tiger!   I don't think you're ready to do that!" So she sat back down.

"Just give me a few minutes and I'll be all right," she said.

"It will take more than a few minutes to straighten you out," he said. She didn't answer; she laid her head back and exhaled in frustration.   The sounds of sirens in the distance grew louder as they quickly approached the park.

"Do you think you could do me a favor?" she asked.   "How about helping me up?   I don't want to look so helpless.   Please Ron, I'm really getting better."   He watched as Grace's lower lip turn inside out with the most pitiful look of begging he ever saw.

"Lady, you remind me of these two mutts, always begging for food with those big sad eyes and pouty little lips," he said.

"Well, does it work?" she asked.

"I guess so," he replied.   He got up and lifted her to her feet.   She was a little wobbly at first.

42

"Could you hand me my pack?" she asked politely. He bent over, picked up her pack, and handed it to her. "Thank you," she said very sweetly. She didn't bring much in the way of makeup and perfumes, but a hairbrush and washcloth were better than nothing. He looked on with the dogs as she cleaned herself up as best she could. "Okay," she said, "I'm ready, let's go." He shook his head and mumbled under his breath. "What did you say?" asked Grace.

"Nothing! I didn't say a thing. Let's go meet some firemen, before they walk all the way down here for nothing." He headed off down the trail. Grace took one step, lost her balance, and fell into a bush. Hearing her scream, he turned in time to see her rolling into the thorny branches and underbrush that straddled both sides of the trail. He ran back to her, "I told you we should wait, and that's what we are going to do!" he exclaimed as he grabbed her by the collar and picked her up with one arm under her legs and the other supporting her neck. He carried her over to a massive stump, some twenty or more feet up the trail and set her on it. She was turning shades of green. Her eyes were watering. She wiped her face with her sleeve.

"I think I'm going to be sick," she said.

"What can I do?" he asked.

Grace looked to the ground in front of her and heaved. Letting out part of the souring remains of her lunch, again she heaved and more came out. She heaved several more times, until her stomach was empty. She was white as a sheet. Ron poured a little water on the face cloth and handed it to her. He piled leaves and debris over Grace's lunch and kept the dogs away from it. She was hopelessly ashamed of herself. What a mess she made of this day. What happened to my sunny morning, she thought to herself? "Ron, I am so sorry. Why is it every time we meet, I am in turmoil? I seem to look as awful as I can whenever you're around."

"I don't know what to say," He answered, "I don't personally cause discomfort, do I?"

"No!" she said, "but I would like to bump into you under different circumstances some time." Ron was quietly thinking about what Grace had just said.

He turned to her and walked over to where she was sitting. He got down on one knee. He took the cloth, poured the rest of the water through it, and squeezed it out. He put his hand up to her face and pushed her hair back. He looked her in the eyes and wiped the moistened cloth softly across her forehead and along the sides of her cheeks, gently padding her nose and eyebrows. She stared back into his eyes as he ran the moistened cloth slowly and softly across her lips, down her chin, and around her neck. He picked up the brush and gently brushed her hair out smooth again. She was mesmerized. He was the gentlest man she had ever met. She asked herself how she became so fortunate to have him there. I don't even know if he has a girlfriend. He stood back admiring his handy work and declared, "I think you're beautiful. I think any fireman would be proud to rescue such a fair maiden." She tried to laugh and nearly choked. "Easy now," he chuckled.

"Hey, Ron!" came a yell from the hill above where they were on the trail.

"That's Moose," he said. "Howdy boys!" said Ron to Moose, Phillip, and Bob.

"Hey, Ron!" said Moose.

"What do we got here?" asked Philip.

"I guess you had a close call, little lady!" said Bob, as he started to take her blood pressure and temperature. "When did you say that pen was going to expire?" asked Bob.

"You know, I never checked for a date! I just assumed they were only good for a year," replied Ron.

"Well, even so, it may not have been expired," said Bob.

"Let me see, I still have it in my pack.   It says use before July of 1981; well, I guess it was still good.   I need to get some more for this year anyway," he said.

"You two out here together?" asked Moose to Grace.

"No," she said. "I was out here alone picking flowers by myself.   One minute I was fine, and the next thing I know I'm waking up with those two dogs guarding me."

"Are those the two dogs you were telling me about, Ron?" asked Bob.

"Yeah, those are the ones," answered Ron.

"Those are good dogs right there, Miss," said Phillip.

Grace was looking at Ron.   "Yeah, they're pretty special," she agreed.

"Well, I think you are going to be fine," said Moose. "Do you think you can walk?" he asked.

"I don't know, I don't think so," replied Grace.

"Let's get you out of here before it gets dark."   Grace was too weak to walk the rest of the way to her car, so the firefighters did what they were trained to do.   Grace was carried out on a stretcher and Ron carried her gear.   Listening to the men talk back and forth to one another for the next hour was quite a learning experience for Grace.

Apparently, Ron was well known to the police and fire departments for his trips into wild country all over the Carolinas; he was single by choice, and everyone knew his dad.   Reno Miller was seventy years of piss and vinegar.   He accompanied Ron on many canoe trips, to some of the most pristine rivers in the Appalachian mountain range.   Reno was known for charming women with his wit and wisdom.   Ron may have been living a saintly life, but Reno surely was going out with a bang.

When they emerged from the trail, and arrived at the ambulance, it was clear Grace was unable to drive herself home. Her Camaro was going to have to be left in the parking lot. As she was lifted into the ambulance, she watched Ron hand her pack to Moose and quietly walk away towards his Jeep. How could he leave without saying goodbye? Grace was so confused. Why did he walk away? She thought he liked her.

Grace was strapped in and the wheels on her stretcher locked down. Moose climbed in back with her gear, and Phillip closed the door behind him.

"Hold on, Miss Grace, this is going to be bumpy until we reach the main road."

"Okay," she quietly answered. Grace stared at the ceiling; she didn't want such a special day to end like this.

Until Moose said, "You know you made quite an impression on that man. I have known him for five or six years now, and I can't ever remember him taking a woman with him into the woods."

"We weren't there together!" she shot back. "I thought I told you that, or maybe it was one of those other guys. Anyway, I was alone when I was stung, and Ron somehow showed up with his dogs and, well…here we are."

"You know he said the same thing, but I think there is something going on with you two. There's a kind of chemistry between you. I could have sworn I saw him brushing your hair when I came over that hill." Grace couldn't help but crack a smile. She turned her head away from Moose hoping he didn't notice, but he started to laugh. "Don't worry little lady, your secret is safe with me." Suddenly Grace was happy things went the way they did. She could not have asked for a better ending to a walk in the park.

Later that night, she lay awake in her bed thinking about Ron. 'Why did he run off like that? When will I see him again? When will I need him again?' Then her thoughts turned to the woods. The memory of

Ron tenderly washing her face makes her thoughts turn to a fantasy of Ron, gently and softly placing kisses on her nose; his warm breath washing over her face.   Chills race through her body.   Passionately they kiss, her body pressing against his, as she runs her hands across his strong back, his heart and hers are pounding as one.   She wants him to make love to her.   He slips off his pants and she can see his hardness through his briefs.   It excites her even more to see that he wants her just as badly.   She slips off her jeans.   He helps her with the buttons on her blouse. They move faster, their excitement building.   They fall back onto the ground and embrace. Kissing and hugging and teasing each other in their private game of foreplay.   And when they can no longer resist, he enters her and she pushes forward to meet him.   Their passions intensify.   They move in the rhythm of love for the rest of the night, until exhausted, they fall asleep in each other's arms.   Grace sighed heavily as she came back to reality. Why did he leave without saying goodbye?   She had a lot to tell Jack tomorrow.   He will never believe me she thought.

Chapter Nine

On the first day of the trial, Grace awoke before her alarm went off. Her clothes were picked out days ago, yet she still wasn't ready to settle for the last choice she made. "Imagine that," she said talking to herself out loud in her bedroom upstairs, "I can't pick an outfit out of all these clothes; I must be losing my mind. Good Lord, I'm talking to myself again. Surely I am going to be in the nut house by the time this is over."

It was summer now and the lawn mowers and weed eaters were clogging the air with dust and pollen. Summer flowers were everywhere. The spring rains came and changed the bleak and barren landscape of winter into the lush and lavish green of a tropical southern summer. The old courthouse was magnificent. Beautifully manicured landscaping bordered every entrance. Freshly painted black wrought iron fences surrounded the walkways and staircases. In the front courtyard facing north, stood a thirty foot tall bronze statue of a soldier standing guard. It was put there shortly after the end of the Civil War. She had been up these granite steps many times in the past few months. She was getting to know the cracks and imperfections by heart.

Today court was in session and Roger Baker was on trial for rape. To maximize the possibility of a conviction, the state decided to have separate trials. Roger and Grace would face each other first. Grace was sitting in the courtroom next to Cindy Conley, one of the four assistants to the District Attorney. Grace hadn't seen Roger Baker since the morning she picked him out of the lineup. She watched all the proceedings in the court room with fascination, absorbing all she could. Throughout the entire process, from the night it happened to this day, Grace had learned a lot about the criminal justice system in North Carolina. She read law books on rape, and even thought about changing her career. Her curiosity for the process kept her more involved than Roger Baker's two other victims.

She shrank in her chair when Roger was called into the court room. A door from the back of the courtroom opened. A guard walked in first; he moved away and stood to one side of the door, while another guard followed behind and stood by the other side of the door, and then Baker entered. Handcuffed and shackled around his ankles, he shuffled towards his attorney at the defendant's table. His court-appointed attorney was a young man; perhaps he was in his late twenties, guessed Grace.

Roger had no money or assets to trade for more experienced council. 'Too bad for him,' thought Grace. He should be so lucky to be born in America, and be given what others in foreign countries can't even imagine. Grace would've liked to return to the days of stoning a criminal in the court square. Innocent until proven guilty beyond the shadow of a doubt — that is what American justice is all about. Grace was going to see that Roger was proven guilty no matter how long it took. Roger looked towards her. His face was red from the blood boiling with hate for her. He didn't say a word to anyone. He sat down in his chair, and a guard chained him to the floor. Roger was not going to get a chance to hurt anyone else.

The court officer rose to his feet, "Hear ye, Hear ye, Court is now in session. All rise for the Honorable Judge Robert D. Savonna." Grace stood next to Cindy; her knees were shaking as her heart raced. Silence painted the room, so only she could hear the pounding in her chest. Her anxiety was eating her up. There were reporters, attorneys, and curious onlookers along with family and friends most of whom were supporting her, but there was one young woman who seemed out of place. She was a well-dressed woman sitting behind Rogers's table. 'Could that be his daughter,' she wondered. 'How must she feel to have Roger as a daddy?' She was repulsed by the notion someone might love and care for such a man, such a monster. She was studying the faces in the courtroom when the Judge slammed his gavel onto the wooden desk top and ordered the trial to begin.

Zachary and Susan sat behind Grace on one of the long wooden benches that filled either side of the court room. Cindy Conley, the assistant to the district attorney, rose to make her opening statement. "Your Honor, ladies and gentlemen of the jury, it is the intention of the State of North Carolina to prove that the defendant, Roger Baker, is guilty beyond a reasonable doubt of the brutal assault and rape of Grace Fields. We will prove that on the night in question, Roger Baker stole a U-Haul from a Texaco station in Green Level, and then drove said vehicle to the Broad Street School where he assaulted the victim, Miss Grace Fields. We will show that Mr. Baker assaulted Miss Fields, and then drove off in the stolen U-Haul, which he then abandoned several miles away switching to his own 1976 Chevrolet pickup truck. We have several witnesses who will corroborate our evidence. Ladies and gentlemen of the jury, we are confident that you will find Mr. Baker guilty of these charges. Thank you."

Grace was staring at the floor as the young court appointed attorney began to speak on Roger Baker's behalf. "Your Honor, ladies and gentleman of the jury; my client Roger Baker is innocent of these charges, and it is going to be proven that the State has accused the wrong man. We believe you will find Roger Baker not guilty."

Chapter Ten

The trial went on for weeks with cross examinations of witnesses. The man from the Texaco station told the court of the night when the U-Haul truck was stolen.   Mr. Slade told the jury about the night he drove to the school to do his job, about seeing the U-Haul parked in the lot, and about seeing a man in the driver's seat.   He thought it was odd, but he had no reason to think that anything bad would happen.   Mr. Slade said he couldn't see who the driver was so he was unable to pick out Roger Baker in the lineup.

The forensic officers testified about how the hairs and fibers found on Grace's body and those at the crime scene matched Roger Baker's hair and how the threads of his woolen coat matched those found on Grace's overcoat.   He wore gloves, but his hairs were found in the U-Haul.   Mud from his shoes was found in the cab of the U-Haul on the floor around the foot pedals.

It was not hard for the jury to take all the evidence against Roger Baker as a sure sign that he was the man who committed the heinous crimes against Grace.   With just an hour of deliberation, the jury came back with a verdict of guilty.   The judge said he would set a date in two weeks for the court to hold the sentencing.   It was believed he would not see freedom for the rest of his life.

Grace and her family spent the next few weeks going about their business without much fanfare.   They were still guarded; it wasn't over yet, and anything could happen including leniency by a liberal judge.

Finally, the day came and the courtroom was packed to capacity. Roger was led in the same way as every day before.   He stared at Grace as he always did.   Grace looked away as before and still shivered with terror and revulsion reliving that night over and over in her mind.

The bailiff entered the courtroom, and for the last time, everyone stood as he introduced Judge Savonna.   The judge cracked his gavel down with a loudness that shook the court windows, not like any time before throughout the entire trial.   He looked over the faces now, seated in their chairs, waiting in anticipation for the end of what seemed forever.   As he began to speak, the entire room was silent. Grace's heart beat as loud and hard as never before.   This was it.   This was the day and moment for which she had been waiting.   Everything she and her family had gone through was coming to an end.

"In the state versus Roger Baker in the assault and rape of Grace Fields, this court has found you, Roger Baker, guilty as charged.   It is the firm belief of this court, and the jury of your peers, that you, Roger Baker, be sentenced to not less than thirty years in a state penitentiary.   As of this day, Mr. Baker, you will, with God's help, never see freedom in your lifetime."   After remaining quiet through the whole of the entire trial, Roger Baker rose to his feet before the deputies could stop him and lunged toward the table where Grace was sitting with the assistant District Attorney.   Even though he was chained to the floor, he tried as best he could to reach for her.   Screaming from the top of his lungs, he promised that one day he would be free and when he was, he would track her down, kill her and anyone she loved.

Grace fell back off her chair, as did the Assistant District Attorney, falling atop of Grace, as they all moved back from the attempts of Roger Baker to get his revenge.

Zachary climbed over the chairs that were in front of him to get to Roger and stop him from reaching Grace.   The deputies that surrounded Roger stopped any attempt at violence from taking place.   The room was full of yelling and mayhem as the judge slammed his gavel again and again trying to regain order in his courtroom.   Through the screams and threats from all the people who hated Roger Baker, the judge ordered him removed from the courtroom.

Six deputies fought and struggled with Roger as they dragged his flailing body through a side door towards the lockup and away from Grace and the rest of the unsettled courtroom participants. Grace was shaking from head to toe, as was Susan.

Zachary reached down and lifted his baby girl to her feet and into his arms. "It's okay. It's okay," he said over and over, as Grace sobbed in his arms, her limp body clinging to his arms for support. "Daddy, please take me home." He squeezed her. As he did, Susan wrapped her arms around her, too. "Let's go home," she whispered into Grace's ear.

That night the news stations were all reporting on the trial, and the craziness that ensued after the sentencing. Grace stayed in her room until the following morning. It may have been the first time in months she slept through the entire night.

Zachary went to work before Grace came downstairs. Susan was cooking breakfast for Alex when Grace entered the kitchen.

"Good morning, Momma," said Grace.

"Good morning, honey. How do you feel this morning?" she asked.

"I feel great this morning. It is over, it is finally over! Momma, I can't believe it is over!" exclaimed an excited Grace.

"Hey, let's go out for supper tonight," said Susan.

"I could go for a hotdog at the Zack's," said Grace.

"Yeah," said Alex. "We haven't been to Zack's since last year."

"You're right, Alex" said Grace. "The last time we went to Zack's was last fall when we came back from the Hillsville Antique Festival.

"Remember that Momma?" asked Grace.

"Yes, I do, and I guess it won't be long before Labor Day again," replied Susan.

Later that day on the way to dinner, the conversation was happy and carefree. Everybody was thinking of the future; the past few months were like a bad dream from which everyone was just awakening.

"Dad, can we go to Hillsville again this year?" asked Alex.

"Well, I guess so," answered Zachary, "but let's wait 'til next month before we make any plans. There's a little bit of summer left; let's enjoy it while we can."

Pulling up to the curb, Susan said, "Zachary, it looks pretty busy in there."

"It's always busy in there, but we always find a table. Don't worry about it, we aren't in any rush," he said as he parked the car. Before he knew it, Alex was running towards the entrance. Zachary yelled after him, "I said there's no rush! Damn that boy, he'll break a leg for a hotdog!"

Grace and Susan walked together to the entrance. Grace was glowing; she could live her life again. Her future was ahead of her and she had a new plan, a new goal. She was finished with Roger Baker.

Alex was already in a booth grinning from ear-to-ear for securing a table. "Boy, you need to relax and wipe that smile off your face. That better be the last time you jump from a vehicle before the damn thing is parked. You hear me?" said Zachary to Alex who was not grinning anymore. "Yes, sir!" he replied.

The girls sat down together and started discussing their orders when the waiter approached the table. He didn't say anything, but looked at Zachary first.

Zachary said, "I will have three all the way, a small fry and a sweet tea." The waiter didn't write anything down, and then he looked at Susan.

She said, "I will have one hot dog all the way, fries and sweet tea."

He then looked at Grace, and she ordered two hotdogs all the way, fries and sweet tea; and then he looked toward Alex who ordered a cheese dog with ketchup only, fries and Dr. Pepper.

The waiter walked to the cook and yelled "Clear! Six dogs all the way, four fries, one cheese dog, ketchup only." Then he made the drinks, delivered them, and went back behind the counter to pick up their food. They were eating within a few minutes.

Alex started to inhale his dog when Susan suggested he slow down and enjoy it. "Alright Momma, sorry," he said.

"Hey Zachary," asked Susan, "isn't that the deputy we met at the hospital that night?" Zachary raised his head from his plate and looked across the room.

"It looks like him," he said, "but his back is sort of turned toward me, so I can't say for sure." Grace wanted to look around to see if it was he, but since the day she was stung, she had not heard from him. She had assumed he wasn't interested. Maybe he was shy and just didn't know how to express himself, but she didn't want to cause anyone any embarrassment trying to find out—at least not here, not tonight.

"Grace, do you think that's him?" asked Susan.

"Momma, I don't want to look. I just want to eat and relax. Let's just leave him alone. I really don't want to look," she replied.

"Well," said Susan, "I guess you know what's best for you better than anyone else."

"Yeah Momma, I guess I do," Grace replied. She concentrated on her hotdogs and tried to stay out of the conversation bouncing back and forth across the table. She sat quietly pondering her future, looking at her momma and daddy across from her. She thought how lucky she was to have them to lean on, to be there for her. Their love was tough at times, but always unconditional. 'How can I ever repay them for all they have given me, and gone through for me,' she thought. She was a woman now, and she knew she owed it to herself and to the two people sitting with her to get back to school to earn a degree and amount to someone for whom they could be proud of. "Momma," announced Grace, "I have been thinking about school, and I think I have made up my mind. I don't want to go back to school and study biology anymore. I want to go to a law school and become a paralegal or an attorney, something that has to do with law and legal issues. I have learned a lot in the past year and I want to learn more. I want to get into the investigation side of crimes and crime scenes. I don't know exactly what it is, I'm trying to say, but I know I no longer want to be a biologist."

"Oh, Grace," said Susan, "We don't care what it is you want to do, as long as you are happy. We will stand by you and help any way we can. Isn't that right Zachary?"

Zachary was looking up at the ceiling fan while she spoke. "What do you mean you want to change in the middle of your college? How? What will...?" Zachary looked at Grace and Susan, sitting across from him, and he knew he had no chance. "Oh don't worry about it. It's okay, we will be all right. You do what makes you happy. Just let me see you graduate from something in the next few years, alright?"

"Alright Daddy, I will. I promise," said Grace, as her eyes filled with tears.

"Hey, here comes that deputy," whispered Susan. She looked over at Grace and said, "I told you it was him."

"Shhhhhh," said Grace and she made a face at Susan that she hoped had displayed the message to let him walk by. "Don't embarrass me, please!" However, Susan was too much of a southern lady to purposely ignore a person, if they were within greeting distance.

"Good evening, folks. How are you Mr. Fields and Mrs. Fields? Miss Grace, Alex how y'all been?" asked Ron as he looked over the family sitting at the table.

"We have been doing fine," replied Susan, "thank you for asking. We never got a chance to thank you for saving our Grace when she was hiking."

"Oh, I was just glad I was able to use my training for a worthy cause," and everyone started laughing. Ron turned to see his friends, Jeremy and Joy. They knew all about the story of Grace and her ambulance ride to the hospital. They, too, were chuckling. Ron pointed to Jeremy and Joy as he introduced them. "This is Jeremy and Joy Faucette. Jeremy is my partner at the Sheriff's Department. He and Joy are also my friends. In fact, I have the title to their pullout sofa. And I donate my expert taste buds at absolutely no charge whenever the occasion arises."

"Yeah, and that's just about every day," exclaimed Joy. And they all laughed together.

"Well, hey, we'll move on so y'all can finish your dinner. Nice to see you again," said Ron.

"It was nice meeting you," said Jeremy.

"Yes, nice meeting you," said Joy. "Hey Grace, I walk at least five times a week in the evenings at City Park. You should stop by some night, and we can chat and work off some room for the next hotdog all the way." Grace looked at Joy for a second, and quickly thought about all the possible meanings what, 'for us to chat,' may mean. Calmly, she replied, "Okay, I'll see you there."

"Great! Bye y'all, and again, it was nice to meet you," said Joy as she ran out to catch up with Ron and Jeremy who were already out the door headed for home.

Grace was speechless, and it seemed as if everyone at the table was waiting for her to speak. 'No way,' she said to herself. 'What just happened here? I think she is setting me up with Ron and everyone knows it.' She finished her hotdog in silence, and kept her eyes down towards her plate. When she finished she got up, and quickly headed for the exit and jumped in the car.   She sat alone for the next few minutes waiting for her parents to come out, replaying the conversation over and over in her head.   'What was I thinking?   What am I doing?   I shouldn't be getting involved with him.   What am I going to say to Joy?'   She made it home without speaking, and ran up to her room and closed her door for the night.

Chapter Eleven

Several weeks later, she mustered the courage to visit the park to look for Joy walking on the oval track.   On this night, Joy didn't show.   Grace walked alone for most of her three miles, but near the end, a handsome softball player caught up to her.   They spoke about college and physical fitness.   Mike was a local kid, who went to Western High School, and Grace graduated from Eastern High; the two schools had a serious rivalry. Mike was stretching his legs for a game he was about to play.   City Park has five baseball diamonds and a soccer / football field.   "Some of the games were pretty intense, you would think it was a matter of life or death," said Mike, trying his best to convince Grace she positively needed to see him and his team kick the butts of their opponent.

"I have to get back home and help momma.   We're going camping for the weekend, and we need to finish packing," she said.

"Oh, I love to camp," said Mike.   "Where are you going?" he asked.

"I guess we'll be going back up to mountains up near the North Carolina and Virginia border.   It is a beautiful place.   We camp and fish along the New River and hike through the mountain trails.   Momma and daddy have been going there long before I was born.   Daddy wants to retire up there, but that's a long way off.   Well, I wish you luck in the game, Mike, but I've got to head on home," she said.

"Hey Grace, it was nice meeting you.   Do you think you might be walking sometime next week?   I have games on Monday and Wednesday nights, maybe you can come by and check one out," said Mike, trying one last time to get her to commit to a meeting.

"Yeah, alright.   We'll see.   Bye!" she said and hurriedly ran off across the field and jumped into her Camaro.   Driving out of the parking lot her skin was crawling, and her legs were shaking as she drove past Mike who was joining his friends. He waved, but she pretended not to see him as she sped away.

When she was home, she told her momma about her encounter with Mike and the feelings that had overcome her when he tried to get closer, trying to get into her life. "It made me feel gross inside," she said. "I now look at my life, and boys or men in a different way. I was afraid to let him get near me. The fear of what he really wants, and how would I explain why it was not possible for that to happen? Momma, I will drag this nightmare around with me for the rest of my life."

"In a way you're right sweetheart. You'll never forget what happened that terrible night, but you don't have to let it take control. You are a strong young woman, Grace. You have the control—you can decide to live your life or watch it pass you by," said Susan. "Already your life's plan has been altered and will continue to be altered. Your future has been dictated by the past as much as anybody's future can be. The question I have about your future is, will you go back to the park and look for Joy?"

"You know, Momma, I think I will cross that bridge when we come back from River Camp U.S.A. Besides, I have gotten accustomed to the peacefulness of being single. I see no reason to change something that isn't broken. You know what I mean, Vern?" Grace said in her best Jim Varney imitation. She giggled and Susan laughed at her silliness. It was a great icebreaker to set the tone for a wonderful weekend of camping and canoeing.

Chapter Twelve

On Monday, Grace worked with Jack on his physical rehab. She kept her experience at the park a secret from him; after all, it was too difficult to even explain it to herself. Jack was mastering the wheel chair and his new van that everyone pitched in to buy for him. It gave him the mobility to travel to appointments and even go back to work while not feeling trapped in his home at the mercy of other people to take him places. He was in love with his new found independence and insisted he drive her to the park, to see if Joy was there. "No," said Grace, "it is still too early. I am going home for a while. Why don't you come by the house around six thirty and pick me up? You can drive me anywhere you want."

"Alright, Brenda and I will be by at six thirty, and I'll have her call you when she gets home from work," said Jack. She left Jack's house and headed home.

She was feeling calm and confident. Jack, on the other hand, was just as nervous as momma, she thought. 'Why are they making such a big deal out of this little thing? Maybe Joy wants to trade recipes, or try to sell me on a plan to save the world. I don't see what the fuss is all about. Besides, if it is to talk about Ron, then I don't have much to say. The man is like a ghost, appearing at some of the most opportune moments, and then disappearing back into the scenery.'

Right on time, Jack and Brenda pulled into the drive and parked the van. Jack was flushed with pride. It was the first time he had driven to Grace's house since his wreck. Zachary and Susan rushed outside to welcome and congratulate him.

"Hey man, when are you going to wash this thing?" asked Zachary.

"When I get a bucket that I can reach the sponge. You know I lose those sponges at the bottom of those little pails."

"I wish you would be a little more careful Jack.   You two should be more serious," said Susan over the embarrassing laughter from Jack and Zachary.

"Hey, Brenda!   How are you?" she asked, trying to change the subject.   "Oh, I am doing fine.   How are you doing?" asked Brenda. "Great!   It's good to see you all out enjoying the evening before the summer ends," said Susan.

Grace came out of the house and said, "Hey, y'all!   Hey, Daddy! Why are you giving Jack such a hard time?   I heard Momma fussing at you from upstairs in the bathroom."

"No," said Jack, "Your Momma is just an old mother hen who thinks she needs to worry about everyone and everything.   Don't worry, Sis, I will be as careful as I can and Zach, I promise to keep this van as shiny as possible, as soon as I find a volunteer to help me."   Jack looked at Brenda and announced, "Hey look, I think I found someone!"   Brenda laughed and shook her head.   "No, I think I will be going on vacation that day!" And they all joined in the laughter.

"Jack, you ain't right," said Grace, "now let's get out of here before Daddy gets started again.   Bye, Momma, I won't be out late, so don't worry."

"Girl, I will never stop worrying about you, or you Mister," said Susan as she pointed to Jack.

"Bye, Daddy, I love you," yelled Grace from the back seat of the van. "Bye baby girl," he said.

Grace, Jack and Brenda headed to the park.   They stopped at a convenience mart for gas and Grace bought a bottle of water.   "I wish I had this the other day.   I was parched after walking the track, and the water out of the fountain was warm and tasted funny.   I am not drinking out of that thing again," she said.

"Do you want us to wait until your friend gets here?" asked Brenda.

"No," said Grace, "If she doesn't come, I will walk the track alone. You can come back in an hour or so to get me. I should be ready to leave by then."

"Alright, we'll see you in a while," said Brenda.

"Thanks, Jack. Try to keep it under 80 mph," said Grace. Jack said, "Oh, come on. That isn't any fun." He spun the tires a little, as he pulled out of the parking lot.

She headed to the track thinking how some things will never change. She walked around the track a couple times before Joy arrived. She watched every car that parked in the lot to see if it was her; and when she did arrive and got out of her car, she immediately recognized her. A five foot eight inch tall, brunette, she was wearing tight spandex shorts. 'I guess she must walk a lot,' thought Grace. 'She is in fantastic shape.' Grace continued walking around the track towards the gate for the parking lot.

Joy was through the gateway and stretching when Grace came up to her. "Hey Grace, have you been here long?" asked Joy.

"I walked a couple laps, but I have a few left in me. How many laps do you usually do?"

"Well, that depends," said Joy "because every night I feel different. I try to get at least nine or ten, since it takes three to make a mile. You look like you keep in good shape."

"I ran track in high school, but I haven't trained for a while," replied Grace.

"Well, you're still young," said Joy.

"Oh, like you're some kind of old lady," said Grace.

"Well, I'm getting up there," said Joy.

"What are you twenty six or twenty seven?" asked Grace.

"Very good," said Joy, "twenty seven last June."

"That's not old," said Grace.

"Well, you tell that to my butt and hips. They have a mind of their own.   I would like to tell you I love to be out walking, but I promise, if I backslide just a little my butt would balloon out."   Grace laughed loud enough for half the park to hear her.   Joy wasn't quite as loud, but she swore she was going to pee her pants from laughing.   By the end of the second lap, it was clear to both women that they were going to be the closest of friends.

"So…" Grace started, "what's the story with Ron?   I keep thinking he and I have a kind of a thing for each other, but every time we bump into each other, he makes small talk then it's like he can't get away fast enough. I don't see or hear from him again unless it's by accident, like the other day at Zack's."

"Well," said Joy and she paused to think of the best way to explain Ron's idea of a proper relationship and improper one.   "Okay, it's like this.   When you and Ron met, you were an exercise in fulfilling his job description and responsibilities.   In other words, he couldn't get involved with a victim or plaintiff in an active investigation because it may have compromised his dedication to professionalism."

"Oh," said Grace, "I see, he likes me, but he can't mix business with pleasure."

"I knew I was going to like you," said Joy, "you hit the nail right on the head, or in this case the cop; and believe me, he has a hard head.   I have known the man for years, and he has been alone the entire time.   He had a few blind dates, but he's never been interested in getting closer than that.

64

I think, however, that the situation is different with you. He's very interested in you, and I know he wishes he had met you on a trail in the wilderness, instead of in uniform investigating a tragedy. Sweetie, I know you went through hell, and so does he."

"So what are we to do?" asked Grace.

"I guess I will have to invite you over as my friend, and let our hard-headed cop come to his senses in his own sweet time."

"Girlfriend, I hope you know what you are doing," said Grace. Joy and Grace made plans to meet the following Saturday afternoon to do some shopping. They planned to surprise Ron and Jeremy with a special dinner.

Saturday finally arrived and the girls put Joy's plan into action. They had their hair done and their nails manicured. Grace broke down and bought herself a new outfit.

Later that evening, after Grace had gotten dressed, she looked at herself in the mirror. She was feeling beautiful and confident. She could melt the icy walls that Ron was hiding behind. Ron was like a brother to Joy and Jeremy. They both wanted him to be happy. Joy hoped Grace was going to be the one to make it happen.

"Hurry, Grace. I think they just pulled into the driveway."

"Okay, I'm ready!" she yelled from the master bathroom. Looking at herself in the large mirror, she could almost see her whole body. She thought, 'Wow, after just a couple of weeks—not bad, not bad. Well here goes nothing!'

Grace and Joy had met at the park nearly every night since that first time and it showed. She could see it and feel it. With her new outfit, and primping for an hour in front of the mirror, she was a knock out; no one would deny it. "Here I come!" she said and she walked into the kitchen, where Joy was busy stirring the meat sauce for the spaghetti.

"Hey! You look amazing!" said Joy, "If Ron doesn't notice, then he is a big dummy!"

"How's the cobbler doing?" asked Grace, as she bent to look into the oven window. "It's almost done.   It smells so good."

"Okay, here they come," said Joy.   She was as excited as a kid in a candy store and couldn't stand still.

"Relax," said Grace. "I'm the one who should be nervous."

"Shhhhh, be quiet," said Joy.

Just then, the front door opened, "Hey, honey! I'm home!"

In silence, Joy and Grace were staring at each other in the kitchen. Joy had her fingers over her lips signaling to Grace to keep quiet.

"Joy, I'm home.   Where are you?" asked Jeremy.   Next, they heard Jeremy and Ron talking, but they couldn't make out what they were saying. Their voices got louder as the two men approached the kitchen.

"Mmmmmm, something smells good," said Ron, as he turned the corner into the kitchen, and stopped dead in his tracks when he saw Grace and Joy dressed up looking like runway models at a New York show.   He stood in silence, his jaw dropping in the most unattractive manner, and then he closed his mouth and swallowed.   Completely speechless, he stared at Grace for what he thought was an eternity, and then Jeremy broke up the silence and yelled from the master bed room, "Hey Joy!   Where are you?"

"I'm in the kitchen," she yelled back, he went to her and saw what Ron was seeing, and he too, was speechless.

"Honey, you remember Grace?   The girl from Zack's; remember you met her and her family a couple weeks ago?"

Jeremy had a puzzled look on his face. This didn't look like the same girl. "You look much different than the first time we met. I didn't recognize you," he said. "How are you?" he asked, as if he thought he needed to keep the conversation going.

"I'm fine," she said. "How are you?"

"Great, just great, um, so... I guess you are having dinner with us?"

Joy came to the rescue and said, "Honey, why don't you and Ron go get cleaned up for dinner, while Grace and I set the table."

"Good idea, I think I'll do that. Come on Ron, old buddy. Let's go get cleaned up for dinner." Ron nodded his head and proceeded to follow Jeremy down the hallway to the other end of the house.

Ron was in shock, "Did you know about this?" he asked Jeremy. "No buddy, I am just as surprised as you," answered Jeremy. "She looks fantastic," said Ron. "Yeah, and Joy looks great as well," replied Jeremy. The two men looked at each other and both were thinking the same thing. "Do you think we are in trouble?" asked Jeremy. "I think these ladies have us right where they want us," said Ron. "Let's get in there and see where this leads. I am curious to know whose idea this little dinner was," said Jeremy. "I wonder, too," Ron thought to himself.

When the two men entered the dining room, Grace and Joy were sitting at the table sipping on glasses of wine and giggling like school girls. "What's so funny?" asked Jeremy. "Well," said Joy, "Grace was telling me about her last camping trip she went on with her parents." "It sounds like you had fun," said Ron, as he sat down across from Grace. Now Ron and Grace were talking face-to-face and his shyness faded away as she began describing the events that took place on her last canoe trip. Ron was hanging on every detail; he had to know more about her adventure. Grace was very much like Ron. They both held a reverence for nature and an appreciation for the peaceful quiet that very few people ever experience.

"My dad always took us on vacations to the mountains," she said. "My brother and I like it better than the beach.   While the kids in school were always bragging about the ocean and amusement parks at the beach, Alex and I were dreaming of fast rapids and steep hiking trails that took you as close to heaven as you could get!   I can still envision looking over the valleys below.   Wow!   My heart is beating fast just thinking about it," said Grace.

"Me too." said Ron.   "I have a trip planned for Labor Day weekend up in the mountains. My dad and I are going together.   We have invited everyone we know as usual, but we sometimes end up going alone," Ron looked at Jeremy and smiled.

"Hey!   Hey! I said I would try," said Jeremy, "you know how hard it is to get time off whenever you want?   Besides, I'm looking for a promotion, and you don't get promoted, if you are always away for the weekend."

"How about you Grace?   Would you be interested in going?" asked Ron.

"I would love to, but I have plans with my family," she said.   "We go to the Hillsville Antique Festival on Labor Day weekend."

"I have heard of that," said Joy.   "My aunt Sophie goes to a lot of antique festivals. She said that it was one of the biggest on the east coast."

"Yes, there are a lot of people there and the venders set up shop all across the hills that surround the little valley.

"I'll tell you what," said Grace, "you spend a couple days walking around that place you better be in shape, because it is something.   I need a vacation after that trip!" They all laughed.

"I think the garlic bread smells done," said Joy, as she got up and headed to the stove.

"Let me help you," said Grace and she followed her into the kitchen.

"Is the cobbler done, too?" she asked Joy as the two ladies looked in the oven.

"I think so. What do you think?" asked Joy.

"It definitely looks done," replied Grace.

"Let's take it out so it can cool while we eat the spaghetti, I hope you guys are hungry," said Joy, "Because we made enough for an army."

"I am," yelled Jeremy from the dining room.

"Me, too," said Ron. "What's the hold up?"

"It's coming! It's coming!"

Grace carried the sauce and Joy brought the pasta and set them on the table.   "Jeremy, would you grab the garlic bread from the counter.   What do you want to drink, Ron?" asked Joy.

"I like milk with my spaghetti, please" he replied.

"Grace, do you want some more wine or milk?" asked Joy.

"I think a glass of milk sounds good, too, thank you."   After everyone had settled at the table, Jeremy blessed the meal and everyone said, "Amen."

"Ron, does your dad bring a friend when he camps?" asked Grace.

"Sometimes, but he usually goes alone.   He says he would rather concentrate on relaxing."

"What do you mean?" asked Joy.

"Well, he says most of the women he knows never learned to appreciate camping.   So he ends up feeling like a babysitter."

"I know what you mean," said Grace, "if you haven't had much experience in the woods, it can be intimidating. Some people can't live without television or toilets."

"Grace, what are you talking about?" asked Joy "your crazy girl."

"No, it's true" she said. "I know some men who would probably die in a week, if they didn't have someone to cook for them or wipe their butts for them!" The whole table shook as Jeremy and Ron broke out in laughter.

"Touché," said Joy, "Put you boys in your place." Grace and Joy gave each other the high five.

The conversations at the dinner table were mostly generic and not too deeply personal. But Grace needed to know more about this man. Why was he so shy? What is it that draws her to this man when she wilts at the thought of any other man trying to touch her?

Joy and Jeremy live in a country farm house that is back off the main road through a winding dirt drive, with a wooden bridge that crosses a small creek and opens up to a ten acre field. From their front porch swing, you can sometimes count as many as thirty deer grazing in the late afternoon as the sun is setting. They come out at the edges away from the house and slowly move out, edging closer to the house as the sun moves further and darkness unveils its glorious blanket of twinkling stars.

"Hey Grace, why don't you and Ron go sit out on the front porch and my darling Jeremy and I will get dessert and bring it out to you."

Ron looked at Grace for approval, when she smiled at him he said, "Sounds good to me." Grace left the table and the pair headed to the front door. Ron reached ahead and opened it for her. "Thank you, sir," she said. As she looked upon the vast field of green, she could feel the late summer coolness sweep across her body; chill bumps appeared on her arms and bare shoulders. "Ooh, it's going to be a cold winter. I can feel it already," she said.

"Hey, let's not rush into winter just yet. I think it's quite comfortable," said Ron. "But wait, I got a plan. I will be right back." He rushed back into the house and returned with a hand crocheted afghan. Grace was sitting on the swing with her arms tucked in tight against her body to help conserve her body heat.

"Hey, that's what I'm talking about," remarked Grace as Ron wrapped her up. "This is a warm blanket; I need one of these at my house," said Grace.

"You remember the E.M.T. that sat in the back of the ambulance with you?" asked Ron.

"Yeah, I think his name was Moose."

"Yes, that's him. His wife makes these in different colors and sizes. Ask Joy about it later and maybe she can hook you up."

"Alright, I'll do that," said Grace.

"Look! Here come the deer," said Ron. He pointed his finger across the field, and Grace followed the line he drew, until she saw the doe and a spotted fawn cautiously following her momma out of the tree line and into the grasses. Soon more followed from around the field, until they dotted the entire ten acres. Ron and Grace settled down on the swing next to each other. Moments passed before Ron spoke. "Grace, I want you to know that I like you a lot. I have tried to forget about you. But I can't. I don't have a girlfriend because of my job. I guess I don't have the confidence that Jeremy has when it comes to women and being a cop at the same time. I don't know if this makes any sense to you."

"Yes, it does," she said. "Ron, I am aware of the danger and possibilities that make your job more than just a job. I'm not asking you for a thing, just for today, just for now, in this moment, you're safe with me, and I am safe with you." Ron was looking deeply into Grace's eyes as her words rolled from her lips. He wasn't blushing anymore. His heart was pounding so hard in his chest he thought it would jump out of his shirt.

"Grace, would you mind if I kissed you?" he asked.   Grace's eyes softened and swelled with tears, she whispered, "No." as they leaned into each other, their lips meeting softly.   Ron pushed in until his nose was tickling the tip of hers.

Suddenly the screen door creaked, and they swung their heads around to catch Jeremy walking backwards with a tray of dishes filled with peach cobbler and vanilla ice-cream.   Grace and Ron sat up straight and acted like nothing had happened.

"Hey you two, ready for this?   I think this is the best cobbler I have ever eaten.   Grace, you really have a knack with a peach."   Grace and Ron sat silently as Jeremy looked at them with his tray stretched out in front of him waiting for each to take a bowl.   He could tell that something was different—that the air was different, something about Ron had changed.   Jeremy could read Ron, like only two cops who have been partners for years could.   Fresh red lipstick wasn't Ron's color and it took every bit of self-control Jeremy had to not make a joke about it.

"Hey, you two want some coffee?" asked Jeremy.

"Sure," said Grace.

"Yes, sure," said Ron, "that would be nice.   Thanks buddy."

"Don't mention it.   I'll be right back, it should be ready."

The screen door closed and Grace looked at Ron.   She asked, "Do you think he saw us?"

No," replied Ron.   "He didn't see anything."   Grace looked at Ron's lips and started to laugh uncontrollably.   She couldn't hold it in, and it felt so good to be able to let go.   Ron was unaware his lips were smeared with ruby red lip gloss.   "What's the joke? Did I miss something?" he asked.

"Let me wipe the lipstick off of your lips," she said, reaching out from

72

under the blanket, she gently ran her thumb across Ron's lips. Ron wiped his hand across his mouth.

"Did I get it? Is any left?"

"Don't worry, it won't kill you!" she laughed.

Ron picked up his dessert bowl, and took out a spoonful of cobbler. He studied it for a moment and looked at her, "Did you put any secret potions, or cast a spell over this stuff?" he asked.

"No," said Grace, and she grabbed Ron's hand and pulled it and the spoon to her mouth, opening wide. She filled her mouth, began chewing, and swallowed it down. Ron smiled in amazement. He reached down and picked up the other bowl, and handed her the spoon she just used. He kept her clean spoon and began to eat from her bowl. "Hey," said Grace "I don't have germs."

"I am not taking any chances," said Ron. The screen door opened and Joy and Jeremy walked out to the porch. Joy walked over to the steps and sat at the arch post on the top step furthest away from Grace and Ron on the swing. She took a deep breath, inhaling the fresh, crisp air. A light fog was forming over the dew moistened grass. "Oh, I love these evenings; so peaceful and comfortable for sitting. This time of the year, we are not so bothered by the bugs." The sky was darkening and the stars were twinkling in the sky. The clearness of the night showed the brightness of the three-quarter moon. "It's almost magical," she said.

"I hate to be a party pooper, but I have early duty. I am going to have to cut out pretty soon," said Ron.

"Oh, come on buddy, stay a little longer," teased Jeremy.

"I didn't say I was leaving now, but I do have to go to bed early tonight. I have a meeting with the boss about the tire store robbery in Saxapahaw."

"Oh, yeah, I read about that in the paper. Did they get away with anything?" asked Grace.

"No, nothing more than a couple of tires were missing.   There wasn't any cash, so it was really just a waste of time.   I think we'll catch them anyway; these guys left behind a lot of clues, and besides, the county's finest is on the job," said Jeremy looking at Ron with a smile.

"Hey, you know what?   We should plan a trip," said Grace. "Joy, what is the best place in the mountains to go if you want a variety of activities a short distance from each other?"

"Well," replied Joy "I think Cherokee would be the best.   You have shopping; camping and gambling, plus you have some of the best hiking on the east coast with the Appalachian Trail not too far up the mountain out of Maggie Valley.   And, you have Gatlinburg and Dollywood just over the border into Tennessee."

"Wow!" said Ron.   "I think there are quite a few trips in that selection of activities."

"I think it would be fun to go on a hike to see some of sights along the way.   We could hike the part of the Appalachian Trail that runs through the Smokey Mountains.   It's in between Gatlinburg and Cherokee," said Joy.   "I have been up there, and the views and rugged terrain will take your breath away.   I always loved hiking through there," she said.   Joy looked at Ron who was staring out at the now darkening scenery.   "Well, Ron, what do you think?   You're the hiking expert?" she asked.

"I think it's a great idea.   We'll have to start by deciding on a stretch of trail, and determine how much time each of us can get off from work all at the same time, and then put the two together and voila we have a plan."

"Wow! You made that sound so easy, Old Swami of the Highland Woods!" joked Grace.

"This is not going to be easy," replied Ron, "but I believe we can do it, and I know it will be worth it!" he said.   "Well, I got to go y'all.   It's past

74

my bedtime, and I really need to be sharp tomorrow. Grace, I had a really good time. I am flattered the two of you girls put this little shindig together for us," he said.

"Come on, let me walk you to your Jeep," she said. "This is a bad neighborhood to walk alone."

"You think it's dangerous here? You should see where old Ron lives in town; it makes our wild kingdom look like a kiddy playground!" laughed Jeremy.

Joy elbowed Jeremy in the ribs.

"What was that for?" he asked.

Joy looked at him innocently, "I don't know what you're talking about."

Ron and Grace laughed at the two of them.

"No, no it's not that bad. There are a couple of bad apples, but most of the folks are trying to make it a nice place to call home. Anyway, I am not going to stay there forever. I have plans to live in a cave in some wooded area away from people like you!" said Ron, and they all laughed.

"Let's get to your car, Ron," said Grace.

"Yeah, sure, let's get out of here before these two corrupt you." Grace followed by Ron's side to his Jeep.

"I was serious about going for a hike," said Grace.

"I know you were," said Ron "and I was serious when I said we would have to train a little before we went. Would you like to start training this weekend?" asked Ron.

"Sure! What did you have in mind?" she replied with a sinister grin.

"Oh, you are such a bad girl!" said Ron. "I was thinking in terms of equipment.   What it is you have, and what you are going to need?"

"Yeah, I know what you meant.   I think anything I don't have my daddy will most likely own."

"I'll give you a call one night next week.   We can put together a to-do list and inventory our gear and supply list."

"Sounds good to me," said Grace.   "Let me give you my number." Ron pulled a note pad from his glove compartment and wrote down Grace's phone number all the while knowing that he had memorized her phone number since the investigation with the hope that he would someday be able to use it.

"So, I'll call you in couple of days," he said.

"Okay" said Grace. "I heard you the first time."   He looked at her and saw she was grinning from ear-to-ear.

"What's so funny?" he asked.

"Well, I guess you're being shy again, because I am waiting for you to kiss me," Grace coyly stated.

"Ouch!   Let's step around to the other side of the Jeep so the neighbors stay clueless," Ron replied as he guided Grace around the vehicle.

"Okay," whispered Grace.   "I won't tell a soul."

"You don't have to whisper," Ron said into Grace's ear, sending shivers down her spine.

She let out a scream that surely scared a dozen or so of roosting doves from the trees above.   Grace buried her face into Ron's chest to muffle her laughter.   She felt like she did the first time she went to the circus as a child with her daddy carrying her; she couldn't control her excitement and anticipation.   Ron was trying his best to cover the laughter coming from his own mouth. "You're going to get us busted," he said to Grace.

Grace put her hand over Ron's mouth and whispered "Hush." When she moved her hand away, their lips came together, unleashing the passion they both had been trying to avoid for so long. Grace was so glad Ron had found her. Ron knew he could go on kissing Grace for an eternity, but he had to get home.

"Grace, I have to leave, but I don't want to let this moment end. I promise I will call you by Wednesday."

"Awwww, I don't want to let you go, but I will if you promise to dream of me tonight," she teased. Ron smiled at her and kissed her one more time before getting into his Jeep and driving down the gravel path.

Grace's stomach rolled with butterflies. Her entire body was flush with excitement—she felt safe and good about herself. She was feeling that little something she had been missing in her life; that little extra you put in your step because you feel like everything is going your way.

Grace walked back to the house thinking she would help Joy with the dishes, cleaning the mess they all made at dinner, but Jeremy and Joy had the situation under control when she walked into the house. Joy and Grace chatted in the master bath about the evening, as Grace changed into her jeans and out of her new dress. They planned to talk more after church the next day.

Chapter Thirteen

Ron drove home from Jeremy and Joy's feeling a little different. He was full of nervous energy and wound up too tightly to sleep. After pacing around the house for what seemed like hours, he finally decided to work out with weights. He had a simple weight bench and some attachments he could switch with different workout routines. Tonight he felt like bench presses. He couldn't come down from the high he got from being with Grace, feeling her in his arms and kissing her soft lips. He pushed himself harder than usual, trying to focus his concentration on something that might put him to sleep. After a couple of sets, he sat up to stretch his back and raised his arms over his head before he strained a muscle. There was a large mirror hanging on the wall in front of the bench, so he could see himself and monitor his technique. He noticed a lump under his arm pit and he rubbed his hand over it. 'I don't remember that being there before,' he thought. And he continued to rub and roll it around until it dawned on him that he was no longer thinking of Grace.

Ron called Grace on Wednesday like he promised. They talked for hours, and planned their first practice hike together after Labor Day weekend, which wasn't far away. Ron and Reno were going on their own adventure while Grace's family was going to the Hillsville Antique Festival. Oh, how Grace wanted to go with Ron and his dad. She hadn't met Reno yet, but had heard a lot about him. 'Good things come to those who wait,' she thought, but the waiting was killing her.

Ron told Reno about the swollen spot under his arm after he left the doctor's office where they took a sample for a biopsy. Reno knew well what this could mean; he lost his wife, Ron's mother, twelve years ago to skin cancer that started out with a lump under her arm. The cancer had reached her lymph nodes and the treatments were ineffective. She suffered in horrible pain and indignity. Never before had he witnessed such cruelty to a human being, than that which was inflicted in the name of saving her life. They tried to keep her alive no matter what the cost. Ron was barely a teenage boy, but he too could feel every needle and all the sickness as if it was happening to him as well. In the end, she begged for the pain to go away. She finally died in a drug induced coma after two weeks. 'We never got to say goodbye,' he would repeat over and over to his friends after the funeral.

Ron had called for an exam the morning after he noticed the lump. With his family history, there was no fooling around and the clinic took him that following day. Grace didn't know yet nor did Joy and Jeremy. Ron thought it best that he get the results before he announced any news, good or bad. This weekend was all he needed to worry about for now. His arm was sore from the needle, and small chunk of flesh they removed was stitched back together. He was not going to let on that he was in pain, and hoped he felt better by Saturday when he would be floating down the New River in a canoe.

"Hello, is Grace available?"

"Ron is that you? It's me," answered Grace.

"Yeah, it's me, what are you doing?" asked Ron.

"I'm just finishing filling out forms for my request to transfer to another school, and I am getting ready to go shopping with my mom to buy groceries for our trip. What are you doing?" she asked.

"I'm going to see my dad to go over our checklist once more before I say we are ready. I guess I just wanted to hear your voice before you left."

"Oh Ron, that is so sweet. I am glad you called. I'm going to miss you too," she said.

"Why don't we get together for dinner Tuesday night? I mean, would you like to have dinner with me on Tuesday?" asked Ron.

"Sure, any way you ask is a yes!" and they both laughed.

"Where would you like to go?" he asked.

"You know, I'm a cheap date. Why don't we go to Zack's? We can dress casual and go for a walk after. I will even buy you an ice-cream cone over at Mayberry's!"

"Sounds great! I have been there before," said Ron. "I'll see you then," said Ron.

"Don't sound so down," begged Grace. "It won't be that long. Besides, you'll be having a ball with your Dad; you probably won't even think of me once you leave the city limits."

"No, you're wrong Grace," said Ron. "I will think of you. I always think of you. You be careful and come back with something no one else has," he said.

"Alright Ron, I will see you in a couple days. Bye!" she said.

"Bye, Grace," answered Ron. As Grace placed the phone back on the wall, she realized she had already found something nobody else had in Ron.

Chapter Fourteen

"Dad, are you ready?" yelled Ron as he walked into Reno's house.

"Yeah, I'm in here," replied Reno.   "How are you feeling?" he asked his son.

"Ah, I'm alright. I guess I'll get by," answered Ron.   "Actually, I can't wait to get up there.   We should see ideal weather conditions for this time of the year."

"I saw the weather reports," said Reno, "it seems that it will be clear and dry for the whole trip."

"You know what I always say?" asked Ron.

"I know.   There is no such thing as bad weather, just bad gear," answered Reno as sarcastically as possible.

"That's right!   Be that way, but don't forget who bails out your canoe when you forget your gear," said Ron.

"Oh, so I forget a bailing bucket one time, and it's like I can't wipe my own ass now.   If your mother could only know the kind of pain in the ass you have become!"

"Alright, let's not bring mom into this.   Seriously, are you all packed? Is there anything I can do to help?"

"No, kid, I took care of everything, trust me," said Reno.

"That's what I'm afraid of," said Ron.   "Alright then, let's get out of here."

Ron and his dad had a three hour drive to Piney Creek in the northwestern part of North Carolina. The drive always gave them time to catch up with the goings on in each of their lives. It was as much a part of the trip as the canoe ride itself. Ron talked about Grace more than anything, and Reno tried not to look too bored. After all, he had not met this imaginary girl. So listening to Ron say, 'I can't wait for you to meet her,' over and over again was starting to give him a headache.

When they arrived at base camp, Reno rushed into the office, ran past Jannis straight for the beer cooler, opened one and drank it down with one breath. Then he grinned at Jannis and ran to her yelling, "I feel great now!", and gave her a bone crushing hug, nearly knocking her over. "How have you been Reno?" she asked.

"I have listened to that boy of mine jawing for hours about some red head back in Burlington, and I am ready to party." Reno looked around and asked, "Where's Ray? I want to see him as soon as possible. I saw a pile of dirt and six camp sites still not finished from last year. What's that bird been doing since I left?"

"Oh, you know Ray, there is always some emergency around here that sets him off track, and then it takes him forever to get caught up again."

"Yep, I know he has too much work and no fun. Let me grab another one of these, and I guess I'll pay you for his brother's, too." Reno downed another ice cold beer in a single breath. "Well, where are you going to park us for the night?" he asked her with the largest grin he could muster.

She said, "I was going to put you across from the showers, but in light of recent events, I think I'm going to put you on the last site down by the river, number thirty-nine, that way, if you get overly happy, shall we say, then no one will complain."

"What makes you think I'm going to be overly happy?" he asked her.

"Because you're already too happy, now!" she said. "Where is Ron, anyway?" she asked as she turned and looked out the window to the parking lot.

"I sent him down to set up camp, and told him I was going to sign us in. He said he would be by to say hello after a while, you know he can't keep his feet out of the water."

"You better get down there and make sure he doesn't set up at the wrong sight."

"I have to tell him? Why me? Why don't you call Ray on the walkie-talkie and ask him to set the boy straight?" Jannis groaned knowing deep down that she would be groaning a lot before this weekend was over.

"Hey, Ray, could you pick up?" A second or two went by and Ray came over the air, "What do you want woman?"

"Could you make sure Ron pitches his tent at site thirty-nine?"

"Site thirty-nine, let me see, he's over here. Wait, oh, here he is. Ron, what site did you want to sleep at tonight?"

Ron looked at Ray and smiled, "Right here, at site thirty-nine," he said.

"I got you covered honey, he's going to pack his stuff and move to thirty nine," Ray said to Jannis.

"Thanks Ray, now your wife thinks I don't know what's going on. I stay at this site every time I come here, and that's where I expected to be staying tonight," said Ron.

"Hey, it gets boring around here, sometimes you have to invent your own fun-and-games," said Ray.

"Yeah, it looks like you played more than worked since I was here last May!"

"Well, it has been a busy year, but not as good as it could have been. I didn't have to rush to get those sites finished because we didn't actually need them."

"It would have been nice to see," said Ron.

"Hey, I have a lot of things to do, not everything gets done the way I want it either. Last year's floods really set us back financially as well as time wise; don't forget we were under water twice last fall. We usually see floods like that once every ten years, but two in a matter of weeks, that was just crazy! All we did last winter was clean up that mess. Then to boot, the state took ten feet away from me along the river's edge for land soil conservation. So, if you want to fish you would be better off going in at the boat launch at the entrance to the campground, and wading through the river to get you back here," said Ray

"Is that why it's overgrown along the banks?" asked Ron.

"Yep, I am not allowed to trim any of the growth along the shore line up to ten feet, and I am supposed to remind folks they can only fish from canoes or down by the entrance," said Ray.

"Wow! That makes it hard for you. I know one of the things that have always made me appreciate this place is the view of the river and fishing from my own site," said Ron.

"Well, you still can, you just have to walk all the way up through the river, and then you have the whole river to yourself," answered Ray. "Hey, here comes the old man. What do you think is in the bag?" asked Ray with a big smile on his face as he looked at Ron.

"What do you think?" Ron shot back sarcastically.

"Hey, you're not your usual self. What's going on with you, Ron?" asked Ray.

"I had a small surgical procedure on a gland under my arm, and it's a little sensitive. The stitches are a few days old, but I still seem to feel them

84

pretty good," said Ron.   "I'm sorry to hear that kid," said Ray sadly.

"I'll be okay.   Just give me some fresh air and sunshine; that's the only medicine I need," said Ron.

"Hey Reno, you old pain in the ass, tell me, is my wife still a virgin or did you have your way with her up at the office?"

"Your lovely wife?   Hell, I made it with her the first time I came here, some eight or nine years ago.   That's old news.   Mr. Ray, how you doing?" Reno asked, pulling Ray into a bear hug.

Fighting for breath, Ray broke loose the clamp Reno had on his chest and said, "Good Lord, what did you have for lunch, a case of beer?"

"Nope, just an appetizer," joked Reno.   "Do you need any help with that, Ron?" asked Reno as the two men watched Ron set up the camp site and pitch his tent.

"No, I can do it," said Ron with a laugh.

"Suit yourself," said Reno, "but make sure you set my tent up in the shade."   I hate the sun cooking my tent while I'm trying to take my nap."

"I can tell what kind of trip this is going to be…" Ron muttered.

Chapter Fifteen

"Oh Grace, look at this collection of salt cellars," whispered Susan in her ear. "Yeah, I saw it," she said "but I was trying to look uninterested until I saw something different. Most of them I already have, so no big deal, yet. There is a lot of nice stuff here this year Momma, but it seems a bit more expensive than I remember in the past."

"Your daddy said the same thing a while ago, I don't see very much of this stuff selling at these prices. Every year, near the end of the last day, prices drop dramatically for a short period of time. Your dad and I were looking at some interesting pieces of furniture made from old barn boards and wood from old structures, real rustic and weather beaten. They just looked so cute; we might buy a piece or two before we go home tomorrow."

"I hope I find something that reminds me of Ron. I want to bring him back something nobody else has."

"What were you thinking of?" asked Susan.

"I don't know, but it has to be so unique that I guess it will just have to find us. Isn't that what Grandma used to say when we came here with her and Grandpa a long time ago? Whenever I asked her what she was looking for she would always say, 'I don't know for sure, but it will find me if I just keep on looking.' She was so much fun, I really miss her."

"So do I, baby, so do I," said Susan staring at the odd looking object with a lamp shade on top. What an odd looking lamp she thought to herself. "Grace, what if you found something unique and useful?"

"What did you say, Momma?" she asked.

"Well, look at that lamp over there in the corner," she said to Grace.

"What lamp?   There's no way that's a lamp," said Grace.

"It looks like a log house someone made out of the same kind of used wood as the furniture I was telling you about," said Susan.   "Isn't it precious?   I wonder if it works."

Grace turned toward the shopkeeper who was watching them admire the lamp.   He started to walk over when he saw Grace look his way. "Yes Miss, I overheard you; it does work and so does the little light on the inside."

"The little light inside?" asked Grace.   Both ladies seemed puzzled until the shopkeeper plugged in the lamp, and on came the inside bulb. Like a magical play toy, the inside of the miniature log cabin was completely furnished with table and chairs, bunk beds, a bearskin rug on the floor, and all kinds of cooking utensils.   There were even pictures and artwork on the walls.   "How much do you want for it?" asked Grace?

"To be honest ladies, it's not going to be cheap," he said.   "I have been asking three hundred and twenty five all weekend, and there have been a lot of folks poking at it you might say, but I'll come down to two hundred and seventy five dollars for you gals."

"Wow that is a lot!   How old is it?" asked Grace.

"I got it from a neighbor in Tennessee; his wife made him sell it when he brought it home from an estate sale at his aunt's.   He said his aunt's father made it to show what his home looked like when he was growing up in the Tennessee Mountains."

"So, this is a replica of a real home from about the 1890s or so?" asked Grace.

"Yes, Miss.   In fact, there is a date and signature on the bottom.   If you just give me a second here, I can show it to you."   The antique dealer reached under the shade grabbing the center support and reached his other hand under the bottom to tip the lamp.   It read *Joseph David Scott*, and the date was 1927.

"Wow, that's pretty old," said Grace.

"Yeah, from what my neighbor said, before Joseph made this lamp, he lived in the hills as a teenager with his family.   There were many families scattered in the high country, little pockets of towns.   There were no doctors to speak of and schools were nothing more than one of the mothers teaching children to read in exchange for whatever she could get – usually it was food.

Anyway, during the First World War, a flu virus traversed the planet on the backs of the fighting men and women.   Believe it or not, the flu hit the people up in the hills hard, wiping out entire communities.   Families of ten or more were often buried next to each other, having died just days apart. Every family lost someone to it.   Joseph and his family had to come down the mountain, to find food and medicine after his daddy and sister got sick. A lot of folks died in these parts, too," added the shopkeeper.

"Yeah, that was a tough time," chimed Susan.   "My mother was alive during that time, and although she was young, she could still recall some of the funerals of the people her parents knew."

"Anyway, that's some of the information I got when I bought it. Who knows if it's true, but it's possible," he said.

"Would you consider taking one hundred and seventy five?" asked Grace.

"Oh, no, I was offered two hundred a while ago and turned it down."

"Would you take two hundred now?" she asked.

"No, Miss, I couldn't possibly.   I'll tell you what.   If I still have it sitting here tomorrow afternoon at closing time, then you check with me, and I'll take two hundred for it."

88

"It's a deal." Grace held out her hand and the keeper reached out and shook her hand to seal the deal.

"Little lady," he said, "I get the feeling you have done this before."

"No, but my daddy sells used cars, so I have learned a thing or two from him. Come on Momma, let's go. I saw some really old gas cans over in the next booth. Daddy might want to check them out."

Grace and Susan strolled out of the tent covered showroom and walked down the dirt road to more rows of covered showrooms, full of antique gas pumps and gas station memorabilia. "I hope you get that little lamp Grace, but it seems a bit expensive, don't you think?" asked Susan.

"Maybe, but it is very unique, and I'll bet it's gone by tomorrow anyway, so don't worry about it. I'm not even going to think about it," said Grace. "I will be careful as to how I spend my money until then," she added.

"Thanks, Ray, I can get it from here," said Ron.

"Okay, kid you're on your own." And Ray gave a last push off the bow of Ron's green canoe, spinning him backwards up stream. Ron pulled his paddle from the water and switched sides. He never lost stride correcting his misguided friend's attempt to rock the little canoe over on him.

"Oh, you wait 'til I get back!" cried Ron, as he floated down the river away from Ray, who was standing knee deep in the crystal clear, cold river. Reno was already a hundred yards downstream. Ron got his gear repositioned and situated just the way he wanted, and within minutes, he had caught Reno, and made his first cast of the day. "Did you see what that nut tried to do to me?" asked Ron.

"No, what did he do?" asked Reno, and Ron looked at him with smiling eyes.

"Never mind," said Ron. "Hey, I bet I get one under that big tree over there," and Ron cast his line perfectly. The two men watched as the current carried the little plastic frog. Ron slowly reeled it in, keeping it looking as real as possible, and out from under the tree, came two eight to nine inch red-eyed bass. "Just what I was hoping for," said Ron. There was going to be good fishing. The two fish followed the frog out away from their shelter. The lead fish made a last second dash for the frog. Ron let up on his line to let the little green frog settle, to slow down for the hungry fish, and it worked. He jerked the tip of the pole and hooked the fish. He reeled it in as fast as he could, and pulled the tip of the pole out of the water. The bass flew through the air and into the boat. "Yeah, that's what I'm talking about!" he yelled. "Where's your pole?" he asked Reno, as he took the hook out of the little bass's mouth, studying the little fish as he slid it between his fingers. "These are nice looking, healthy little bass. Where is your pole Dad?" he asked again.

"I broke the damn thing when I packed it in the car to come up here. Don't worry about me, you just fish and I'll watch," barked Reno.

"Well, you can use my pole anytime you want," he said.

"I know," said Reno, "but you got that little frog dancing real nice. Why don't you enjoy it, before I lose it on you?"

"Yeah, you're right," said Ron "you do catch more limbs than fish. By the way, how's that hangover treating you?"

Chapter Sixteen

"Hello, is Grace available? This is Ron."

"Oh, hello, Ron, this is Susan. How have you been?"

"I've been fine Mrs. Fields. How are you and Mr. Fields?" Susan could feel the uneasiness in Ron's voice. She could tell he was feeling a bit self-conscious about dating Grace. He never dated anyone he met during police work.

"Ron, Grace is at the park with Joy. They went for a walk. She hasn't been gone long; maybe you can catch her over there."

"Thank you, Mrs. Fields." "Please, Ron, call me Susan, unless you want me to call you Officer Miller."

"Yes, Ma'am, I mean, no, Ma'am, I don't. Thank you, Miss Susan, you're very kind. I will check the park. Thank you," he said.

"You're welcome Ron," she answered.

Ron drove to City Park to find Grace and Joy. He figured it was a good time to tell them both about the tests on the lump under his arm. Pulling into the parking lot, he could see Grace and Joy walking side-by-side at the far end of the track heading in his direction. He hurriedly closed his door and jogged to the gated entrance to the park's fields. Two teams were already on the field. It was a championship game between Haw River Flooring and Hunt Electrical Services. There were large crowds on both sides of the field. The people on the third base side were cheering for a player who was rounding second base and headed for third. He slid into the bag and was called safe on a close throw from the right fielder.

Ron thought of his days in high school when he played for Coach Thompson. He was a great coach and Ron had loved playing baseball back then. Coach Thompson was one of the reasons Ron went into law enforcement. He was troubled after his mom died of cancer, and the coach was the one who introduced him to Scout Master Donald Kinney. Mr. Kinney was a scout most of his sixty-seven years. He knew how to keep a young man's attention while sneaking in a lesson or two when he was not looking. Most of all, he taught Ron the value of discipline, how to set a goal and achieve success through focusing on the task and never giving up. Now Ron could be facing the greatest battle of his life.

As the girls approached, their faces lit up as they recognized it was him. They started to slow down, but Ron jumped in next to Grace with his feet running in place and said "Now let's go, let's see what you got." And the three of them sprinted down around the corner to the back stop. Grace and Joy were purposely keeping back as Ron pulled a head. Grace looked over at Joy and said, "Are you ready?" through her huffs and puffs.

Joy yelled back "Let's do it!" The girls raced forward catching Ron and pulling ahead, taking Ron by surprise, he started to laugh and the girls started to laugh, too. He raced forward and pulled back up to them, as he started to pull ahead, they all slowed down after the hundred yard marker, and jogged a little more just to cool down. "Damn," said Ron, "I need to get back out here more often. Y'all almost handed my butt to me!"

"Oh, we could have taken your butt. We could tell you were about to burn out, and we were going to fade away right on by you."

"That's right, Joy, you tell that old fart what's up," said Grace.

"Okay, you win. Let's go sit at that picnic table over there," said Ron.

"No sweat, grandpa. How about we race to it?" asked Grace.

"No, I just want to walk," he replied.

"What brings you down here anyway?" asked Grace.

"Well, I wanted to talk to you, and since I need to give Joy the same report, I figured I would get two birds with one stone so to speak." Joy knew Ron far better than Grace, and she could tell he was about to share something with them she wasn't going to like.

"What's wrong?" she asked him.

"Well, Joy, as you already know, my mom died of cancer when I was a kid. They say she got it from a mole on her back. Well, things are better today with all the medical advances." Ron looked at Grace as he spoke, "Anyway, to make a long story short, I have a little spot on my shoulder that may be cancerous. I don't have anything wrong with my glands, because I had a piece of it removed and tested. That's why I am here. I just got the results back today."

Grace was turning pale. He could see the blood leave her face. She could not move as he told the story of his biopsy.

"I have to go to a specialist in the city, a Doctor Ingall. He's to search every inch of my body, and remove anything he thinks is suspicious, and then have everything individually tested and a lot of other tests, but they believe I came in just in time and I should have a very good chance of being cancer free."

Grace broke down and fell towards Ron. He reached out and grabbed her, saving her from passing out and cracking her head on the ground. He lowered her down slowly. She regained her senses and said, "Oh, my legs went numb. I tried to go to you and I blacked out for a second. Oh, Ron, I'm so sorry!" said Grace.

"I am going to miss a lot of time in the woods with you, at least for a little while," he said.

"Don't even worry about that, we just have to help you get better so we can all go on that trip to Newfound Gap in the Smokies," she said.

"Yeah, that's going to happen, I can feel it!" said Ron.

"Well, at least we won't be lacking in positive attitudes," said Joy, "that's you all the way, Ron.   Never let anything get you down; just keep on smiling," said Joy as she gave Ron a hug.

"So…what do you want to do tonight, Grace?" asked Ron, "I am going home and getting changed out of these clothes," he said with a sheepish grin.

"Don't try to change the subject," she said, "I know what you are doing," said Grace through her sobs as tears rolled down her cheeks. "You can't just drop a bomb like that and expect us to go on like nothing is really happening.   I'll tell you what we're doing tonight," she said, "I am going to meet you at your house later on around 8:30.   My mom and I found something in Hillsville that is one of a kind.   You will not find another one like it.   I was going to wait for Christmas, but I think today is going to have to do."

"I can't wait," he replied.

Chapter Seventeen

Grace was full of emotions. She had never felt like this before. They had been riding a roller coaster since they first met. With the investigation and trial out of the way, she had hoped her life would return to normal and they would grow closer without the drama she had been enduring for so long. They had barely known each other a few months, but the time they had spent together could fill a lifetime with special moments. She thought about the time in the woods, when he and his dogs came to the rescue and how he was so gentle and the night they first kissed on Joy's front porch, in the dimming sunlight overlooking the field, and later when they kissed each other good night. Grace could feel goose bumps spreading across her back and down her arms. As she dried her hair, she thought of the night to come, it had to be special. They went to Zack's for dinner a couple times, and had breakfast once, but she still had not met his dad or been to his house.

This was going to be the first time in Ron's home. I hope he likes his gift, she thought as she left the driveway of her own home, and headed off to his. Spruce Street in Burlington is not that far, but Grace had a lot of time to consider all the possibilities and complications Ron might be facing. She knew she could help him if he would only let her.

Using Ron's directions, Grace found the little brick house with relative ease. Pulling into the driveway over the broken and cracked pavement, her Camaro spun a few stones onto the street behind her. Ron chuckled to himself watching from the picture window facing the front yard and road. 'The neighborhood just went up in value,' he thought to himself.

She parked next to his Jeep, and stepped out onto the pea stone covered lot. Magic and Boo were at her side by the time her door closed. She had not seen them since her hike at Cedar Rock Park. "Hey, girls, do you remember me?" she asked. Both dogs were wagging their tails excitedly. Grace took that as a yes, and got down on one knee to let both dogs lick her face as she stroked their backs and rubbed on each one's ears. Both dogs tried pushing the other out of the way to get all of Grace's attention. Boo growled and moaned at Magic and pushed her nose into her thick black fur until she backed up. "You two have to share," laughed Grace as she played with Magic's ear. Boo tried to get her nose under Grace's other hand, which was on the ground trying to help keep her balance. "Okay," she said to Boo, "I get the point," so she got onto her feet and bent over to rub both of them at the same time. Both dogs were talking to Grace, moaning and groaning, like her daddy did when her momma rubbed his shoulders when he came home from a stressful day at work. "Okay girls, where is your master?" she asked.

Grace looked up towards the back of the house; there was a covered porch, and the door was closed. Coming up the sidewalk, she marveled at the stone fountain that sat in the center of a circular cement patio outlined with shrubs and flowerbeds. Magic and Boo walked beside her like proud princesses entering the ballroom. Coming closer to the fountain, she could see gold fish swimming about the top of the little pond. She stood and watched them for a moment, and then she heard the back door open.

She turned around to see Ron standing in the doorway. He had never looked more handsome she thought. He was wearing a thick, light green fleece sweatshirt with a zipper at the neck and an extended collar, and a bluish green turtleneck shirt under that, khakis and hiking boots. He had his tan colored Tilley hat on his head, and his face was clean-shaven. "Wow! I'm impressed," she said, as he stepped off the back porch, and started to walk towards her. He was unsure of himself, and he was nervous and didn't want Grace to feel any pressure. So he walked off to the side of her and stood next to the fountain.

Staring into it, he asked her, "How many fish do you think I have in here?"

Grace leaned forward and stared at the little pond. She gasped as her gaze focused on a small school of guppies that seemed to appear from nowhere.   Then she pointed to a school of black fish a little bigger than the guppies, "What are those?" she asked Ron.

"Those are mollies. There must be at least thirty of them swimming around in there."

"You are kidding me?" she said.

"No, really," said Ron.   "I'm serious.   They are called live breeders, which mean they don't lay eggs.   The baby mollies are ready to go at birth, just like those guppies," and he pointed to the school of guppies that appeared and disappeared back to the bottom as they fed on the plants that grew along the sides and bottom.   "I have about a hundred fish in this little pond."

"You got to be kidding me?" she said.   "I am even more impressed."

"Yes, there are even crawdads in there."   Ron paused and thought of what he was missing, "Oh, and there's some algae eating fish.   I don't get to see them much, except for when I release them after I buy them. There's a couple of frogs that come out on those lily pads, and sit waiting for flies to land, so they can shoot their sticky little tongues at them.   I have seen some frogs catch as many as four in a matter of minutes, just by slowly turning their body, never actually moving from their original spots; but it is getting too cool for the frogs and flies to be around now.   Maybe in the spring, you can sit with me and we can watch all the action together.

"In early summer tree frogs come in to lay their eggs and that to me is the best part of having this little pond in the back yard."

"Why is that?" Grace asked.

"Well," he paused, "during the hottest months of the summer, this is the only place for water this little part of the neighborhood has.   Once the creeks from the spring runoff dry up, the only place for permanent water is here.   Then the eggs hatch out into tiny pollywogs that grow to several inches before they sprout legs and jump out.   This place gets very loud and busy with screaming tree frogs every night until winter comes back and they disappear again.   An added bonus is that birds drink out of it when it gets hot and dry.

"I am still looking for the right snapping turtle to let loose in there. One of my homeless friends has brought me several turtles, but each one was too big or not a snapper.   So I returned them to the wild across the road at the creek.   Maybe if I stop trading him the turtles for sandwiches, he would stop bringing every one he finds, and just get me the one I want!"

"You give him sandwiches every time he brings you a turtle?" she asked, with a look of dismay.

"Well," said Ron, "I don't want to pay him with cash; he'll just buy drugs. Usually you are bothered more if the word gets out that you have a soft heart and aren't too bright, so it could be worse."

Grace looked around the neighborhood from where they were standing.   "My little section of town has bigger homes, most of them are brick.   Our house is vinyl sided.   It isn't as new as some of the others. We have a barn in the back of the house and a big field in the back yard. It was a big joke when we were kids.   All our friends would say 'hey let's go play at the Field's field,' really fast, and it would sound funny.   It's kind of funny now, but back then, it was just kids teasing each other.   My dad put in a pool for us and at one time, we had a couple of horses and a pony in the field.   But my dad worked himself to death trying to keep it all up. When we got older, my folks bought a lake house on Buggs Island.   We didn't spend as much time around the house after that, so my dad filled in the pool, and we sold the horses and all the tack.   Some of those houses could use a makeover," she said as she looked around.

"That's a good way to put it," he laughed.

"Did you build that, too?" asked Grace, pointing to a white vinyl sided storage building at the end of the driveway.

"Yeah, me and some buddies put that up.   I have a fairly useful workshop in there," he said.

"You'll have to show me sometime," she said playfully.

"No problem, Madam, it will be done," he said with a foreign accent. Grace laughed and they accidentally bumped into each other in the nervous, jittery dance they were doing beside the fountain in the back of Ron's yard. They looked at each other and stopped. Grace and Ron embraced and held each other tight. Ron was squeezing Grace as hard as he could without breaking her in two. Grace could feel the strength in his arms, and melted into him like butter on a hot skillet. "Oh Ron, I'm so proud of you," she whispered in his ear. "Anyone would be happy to call this home. Even with all the broken down houses around you," she said, and the two of them laughed out loud.

"Well, it's not forever. As soon as I win the lottery, I'm going to buy some land and build a log house. First, I have to get a few moles taken care of, and I shouldn't have any problems after that."

"Oh Ron, I hope and pray that's all it is. And I'll do anything I can to help; all you have to do is ask. I'll be right here."

"Come on now; let's not get too dramatic; I will be fine. In a couple of months, I will be cancer free, that's what the doctors are telling me, so I'm not worried. My doctor, who recommended Dr. Ingall, said he was the best in the area at treating the kind of skin cancer I have. So let's not even think about it tonight, okay?"

Grace felt the frustration in Ron's voice. He had no control over his life. Since his mom passed, he had been on his own. Reno was no substitute for a mother. Ron was gradually, yet cautiously, accepting Grace's mothering instincts playing a part of their life. Grace was just as aware as anyone could be that Ron was proud and not used to someone taking care of him—certainly not a woman who loved him as much as any mother.

"If I need any chicken soup, you will be the only one I will allow to warm it on the stove for me," he said mocking her candor.   She punched him in the arm, and he winced at the sharpness of her knuckles.   "Ouch, that hurt!" he yelled with a hint of laughter in his voice.   "I thought you wanted to take care of me?" he asked.   "Now I have a new bruise.   What kind of a nurse did that agency send me?"

Grace was giggling, "I'm sorry," she said, "I'll behave, I won't burn the soup as long as you're a good patient."

"It's a deal," he said, and they shook hands on it.   "Would you like to see the inside of my house?   The outside is probably better, but it's getting dark and cold out here."

"Okay, but wait I forgot something in the car.   Could you help me carry it in the house?" she asked.

"Sure, what have you got?" he asked.

"Nothing, just a box," she replied.

"What do you mean just a box?"   "What's in the box?" he asked.

"It's a surprise, so let's bring it in the house and you can open it."

"Now, why did you go and do that, it's not Christmas or my birthday? You really shouldn't have done this."

"Just carry the box, Ron," she said in a joking manner.

"Yes, Madam." he replied.   Ron set the box on the kitchen table as Grace entered the little house behind him.   She was not surprised by the way he had decorated it.   He said, "Look around, you can ask about anything you want, only if you are not afraid of the answer being different than the one you wanted to hear."   Grace walked into the living room in the front of the house.   There was a large picture window that gave a view of the street below and the valley with its creek which ran behind the houses on the other side of the street.   "That trailer park in the distance really adds a touch of charm to this otherwise perfect picture," she said.

100

"What trailer park?" he asked, "I've never seen a trailer park out there," he yelled back from the kitchen. She could hear the clanking of glasses, and cabinet doors opening and closing from the kitchen. "Do you want something to drink?" he yelled to her.

She answered from behind him, "You don't have to yell anymore, and, yes, I would," as she leaned against the counter next to him. "What do you have?" she asked.

"I have orange juice, water and milk."

"Water is good," she said. That's when Grace noticed Ron didn't have a normal sized refrigerator. It was just a little freezer and a college dorm room sized refrigerator sitting next to it. "Why do you have such a small refrigerator?" she asked.

"You probably would find it silly, but I am trying to save money, and these two units together are easy to move and cheap to run. I really want to buy some land and move out to the country. Anything I can do to save a dime to go back in the bank; I am going to do it."

"I understand. Okay, now open the box," she said. Ron started to pull the paper off the three-foot tall cardboard box. Looking at Grace he mumbled some words to her that she couldn't understand. "Just keep going wise guy," she said. Ron got the paper off and pulled the top flaps up very carefully so as not to damage any of the contents.

"What's this?" he asked as he lifted the lamp out from the box and set it on the table. "Wow! That's pretty cool, does it work?" he asked.

"Of course it works," she said. "Let's find a home for it and plug it in. You have a bookshelf in the living room. I'll bet it will fit there, and there is an outlet on the wall behind it," said Grace.

"Boy, you know more about my house, than I do," he said. "Did you ever consider becoming a detective?" he asked.

"No, I think I'll stick to my own plan," she answered.

"By the way, how is that going?" he asked.

"Well, I haven't been accepted to a school yet, but I am still trying. Some of the applications are long and require essays, questionnaires, interviews and of course, the all-important cash. My dad is being patient, but I know he wants me to get back to school. Maybe it's because of all those years of biology classes and preparation for college. I mean, that is what I wanted to be all my life. I guess it's hard for people to see me as a crime scene investigator," said Grace.

"Well, all that biology and chemistry will still come in handy, and maybe we will bump into each other on the job," said Ron.

"Yeah, well, that could take years and who knows; I might end up in an office, and never even get to go out in the actual field. Anyway, let's plug this baby in and see what it does," she said. Ron and Grace took the lamp into the living room and made a space on top of the little bookshelf.

"I think this is a good spot," said Ron, as he plugged the lamp into the wall, and slid the bookcase back into its original position. Grace turned the knob under the lamp, and on came the light and the little lamp that resembled a house from the Tennessee Mountain's glowed magically before his eyes. He peered into the windows and door and gasped at the intricate workmanship and detail. "Wow! I'll bet this must have taken some time to put together. Look at the little furniture. This is awesome! Where did you get this?" he asked.

"Well, it came from the antique festival, but the man we got it from said it was an authentic replica of an old house from the late 1800s. Every time I look into it, I see something new. It is truly unique. Is it not?" she asked.

Ron looked at Grace and said she was truly unique. "No, I mean the lamp is unique," he said. "Hey, I am a good judge of what is unique, and you my lady, are unique."

"Yeah, you think so?" she asked.

"Yes, I do," he replied.   As he moved closer to her, he took his hand and softly moved her hair back from her face.   Looking into her eyes he said, "There, now I can see all of your beautiful face."   Grace shivered from his touch.   Her arms were exploding with goose bumps.   Ron pulled her close and they kissed softly, slowly.   She melted into his arms. She had been waiting with anticipation for this moment to come.

"Ron, I am so happy right now, it's like a dream and I never want to wake up," she said.

"I know, I feel it, too," said Ron.

"Do you remember what we talked about on Joy's swing, the first night we kissed?" she asked.

"Yes, I do," he answered, "Why?"

"Well, for tonight I am safe with you, and you are safe with me, and nothing is going to hurt us.   Just for tonight, let's forget there is a world outside these doors.   I just want to stay in your arms and have you in mine.   Ron, I want to be with you more than I ever wanted anything in my life."

Ron squeezed her as hard as he could, and she could feel his hardness as she pressed herself closer to him.   They kissed more deeply than before with more passion than any kiss they had ever shared.   She ran her hands over his back and down to his hips; she pulled him closer and ground her hips into his.

"Ron, I want to see your bedroom, let's go to your bedroom," she begged.   He was nervous with anticipation and nearly tripped over his own feet as he turned to lead her to the room at the end of the hall.   The shades were drawn and the room was dark.   She said, "Leave the lights off."

"Okay," he said.   "Do you mind if I light a candle?   I have one in the kitchen."

"Yes, a candle would be good, but hurry!" He left her in the darkened room and ran to the kitchen turning off all the lights and locking the doors on his way back.

"I hope this will be okay; it doesn't have a special scent, but it will do in an emergency."

"Ron, is this an emergency?" she asked as she reached for his belt before he could finish striking the match to light the candle.

He inhaled sharply from her touch. "Ohhhh, yes, I think it is," he replied setting the burning candle on the nightstand before he dropped it. She unbuckled his belt as he pulled his shirt over his head. He shivered as the coolness of the air hit his overheated body. She had his pants sliding down in seconds, her arm brushed against his swollen manhood. She was as excited as he was. He tried to step from his pants, but tripped on to the bed. "Wow!" he yelled, "maybe I should take my shoes off first." As he sat on the bed and clumsily removed his shoes and pants, she pulled her dress over her head, and stood before him in the candle lit room. "Man," he said, "what have I done to deserve this? You are a vision of beauty. I've been waiting for you all of my life."

Still sitting on the bed, he pulled her to him and kissed her belly button, sliding his tongue up her stomach as he slid her panties to the floor. She gasped as his hand brushed her inner thigh. He lay back on the bed pulling her along with him. She fell forward and came to rest on top him. They kissed, stroking each other, exploring each other's bodies. He snapped at her bra strap trying to release the gifts that hid within. Like a child with a new toy, he fumbled until the clasp was free. He rolled her off of him and lay beside her, hungrily suckling the nipples that filled his dreams on the many nights since they had first met. She was moaning with the pleasure his gentle teasing was giving her. She stroked his hair and rubbed the back of his head. She could feel his throbbing heat pressed against her thigh. He lifted himself over her and kissed her forehead, chin and cheeks, brushing his lips along the sides of her face and blowing whispers of love with every breath he took. He tenderly massaged her face with only the gentle touch of his lips. She reached her

104

arms around his lower back and pulled at him as he hovered over her. He stood his ground, teasing her even more. She lifted herself to him until she felt him push into her. She ground her hips into him and pulled him down as her legs spread to meet his fullness. He pushed in slowly, what seemed like an eternity, and slowly backed out before fully penetrating.

He could feel her sighing with the anticipation of feeling all of him deep inside her. Yet, he continued his playful tease until he could stand no more and pushed deep into her, kissing her passionately, slowly making love to her and fighting to keep from exploding. "You make me feel so good," he whispered in her ear. She shivered when his hot breath filled her ear and shot through her body making her orgasm roll from her toes to the tips of her fingers. She squeezed him as tightly as she could, wrap her legs tighter around his hips, and he came with an intensity he never experienced before. They held each other tightly, kissing and gasping for air.

"Ron, I have fallen in love with you. I am so scared for you. I would die if I lost you now."

He squeezed her tight and whispered in her ear, "I love you too," and kissed her fears away as they made love again.

The next few weeks went by quickly. Grace and Ron spent all their spare time together. They explored the trails together and practiced using their hiking equipment. They were going to hike in the Smokey Mountain National Park in the spring. It was going to be their first big adventure together. Grace was so excited, and she was happy. She was totally and completely in love with Ron, and he was with her. All of the turmoil of the past seemed like a lifetime ago. Jack was settling into his life and accepting his limitations. Grace found a job at a music store. She was starting classes after the New Year. Everything was falling into place. It was late in the fall now. The leaves were turning and the morning air was crisp and the fog hung through the trees.

It was the first Saturday in October. Grace and Ron were hiking a trail they had been on many times before.

"Grace, did you see the moon last night?" asked Ron.

"Yes, I did.   I sat on the swing at Joy's house after I got off work," answered Grace.   "We wrapped up in blankets; it was a little chilly last night, but it sure was bright. I cannot remember the last time I did something like that.   It was definitely big and bright.   Why?   What were you doing when the moon shined so bright?" she asked.

"Well, I was on the road, trying to keep the drunk drivers from killing themselves and the rest of us.   But, I kept looking up at the sky.   It sure was bright.   I kept thinking of you and what you were doing.   I knew you were working, but I just wanted to be with you.   That's what I was doing, and that's what I was thinking," said Ron.

"Oh, that's so sweet.   You know Ron, I think you're finally coming out of your shell," she said.

"So how many times do you want to hike this trail?   We are almost done." he asked.

"Well, I guess we could do another lap.   What's another three miles?" she answered.   "What do you want to do for dinner?" she asked.   "We could get some stuff at the grocery store and cook at my house, or we could go to your house, and put a steak on your grill."

"Well, a steak sounds good. I have not had a steak in a while.   I think the grill needs a workout, anyway.   So let's do it.   Let us head over to my house when we get off the trail and I can entertain you and relax.   We can even light a fire in the chiminea.

The fact that Ron had an appointment with Dr. Ingall Monday morning never came up the whole weekend.   Their hearts could not bear the pain of thinking of the possibilities.   Dr. Ingall was supposed to be the best, and if there was anything that was wrong, he was supposed to be able

106

to fix it.

Chapter Eighteen

Monday morning at 9:00 a.m., Reno pulled up in front of Ron's house. He parked his truck and sat there waiting for Ron to come out. Reno was nervous for his son. He thought back to the past. Many years before he had the same fear and sick feeling in his gut when he drove his wife to the doctor for her first visit to try to remove the cancer that ended up taking her life. Then as now, he was hopeful and prayed for God to cure his son.

Ron heard Reno's truck pull up to the house. He looked out the picture window to see his dad with his head hung low, a look of fear and sadness on his face. Ron knew this was going to be hard on his dad. He closed the door behind him and walked down the sidewalk towards the waiting truck. Magic and Boo were standing on the hill that looked down to the road. As Ron walked down the steps to the road, he looked toward his dogs and smiled. Reno saw his son approaching, and as he watched him walk down the steps he could not help but feel relieved as his son smiled at his dogs. Surely, the world was a better place with his son in it. Ron climbed into the truck and buckled himself in; he looked at Reno who was smiling to himself.

"What is so funny?" asked Ron.

"Nothing, my son, nothing at all! So how's that little girl you been running with?" he asked.

"She is fine," he answered. "She is quite a woman, Dad."

"She must be. I haven't seen nor heard a word for weeks until this weekend, so I guess she must be something. I do not think you dated anyone this long since you graduated from the Academy."

"Well, you know I have my priorities. Besides Dad, she is everything I dreamed I wanted in a woman.   The only thing that would be a problem is this. I am not sure what this visit will find or how it will affect my future. However, I cannot worry about it now.   Let's just wait until the doc checks me over and go from there."

The ride was short, but the silence of wonder made it seem like an eternity.   As Ron entered the door to the hospital, he thought back to the night he met Grace.   She was wrapped in a blanket and shivering in shock. Now, it was his turn to face the demons of life.   She beat her enemy back with courage and dignity.   Her strength would be his beacon to follow.

They stepped up to the reception desk. "Hi! My name is Ron Miller," he said. "I have an appointment with Dr. Ingall."

"Yes, Mr. Miller. Please sign in on this sheet, and take this to fill out the questions to the best of your ability," said the receptionist.

"Yes, Ma'am," answered Ron.

The two men sat together as Ron filled out the questionnaire. "Wow! Some of these questions are tough.   When was your last visit to the doctor?" he joked.   "Do you take any drugs?"   "Does aspirin count?" He chuckled and looked at Reno.   "What about you Dad, when was the last time you took any drugs?"

"Well, does Spanish Fly count?   Because I took one of them just the other night," he replied.

Ron burst out laughing while Reno looked at him with a serious glare.

"You wait. Your time will come.   Things don't always work the way you want them to."

"No, Dad it's not that. I just can't imagine you being in that position, as it were."   Ron continued to laugh as he filled out the questionnaire.

"Yes, well you keep laughing," whispered Reno.

Then Ron got a serious look on his face, and paused as he thought out loud. "I hope I live long enough to need it," he said.

Reno looked at him and then said, "I hope you do too son.   I hope you do too."   The two men didn't speak for the next few moments waiting for the receptionist to call his name.

When he was called, he rose with a nervous shaking in his knees.   He was not one to fear anything; he had been face-to-face with criminals intent on doing him harm.   He even stood down a black bear in the backcountry on a backpacking trip in the Berkshire Mountain Range in northwestern Massachusetts.   But this was different; he couldn't cuff it, and put it away behind bars or scare it away with the high pitch sound of a whistle.   This was a fear he had never had to face.   The two men walked through the swinging doors and down the hall to another reception area.

The nurse asked if he was Mr. Miller. "Yes," answered Ron.   And the nurse said, "One moment please," as she pushed a buzzer that allowed the door that led to the exam rooms to open.   As they walked by the nurse in the reception cubicle, she told them to enter room number five and the doctor would be in to see them in a few moments.

"Yes, Ma'am," said Ron. They walked down the hall to exam room five.   Ron sat on the stool and Reno sat in a padded chair that was behind the door.   Both men studied the paintings on the walls, and the array of medical tools and utensils, which were neatly placed upon the counter. The silence was broken when a tall, wiry man in a white coat entered the room and closed the door behind him.   He looked down at Reno as he turned to Ron.   "Hello!" he said, as he looked down at the chart in his hand.   "Mr. Miller, I am Dr. Ingall."

"Hi, Doc," said Ron.   "This is my dad, Reno Miller."

"Okay, so you're the patient," he said looking at Ron.

"Yes, sir," answered Ron.

"Okay, would you jump up on the exam table for me?"

Ron got up off the stool and sat on the exam table while the Doc sat on the stool. "Tell me, Mr. Miller, what did the dermatologist tell you about your biopsy?"

"Well," said Ron, "he said that he didn't think that the biopsy was cancerous, but that they thought it would be a good idea to come to you for a complete physical."

"I see," replied the doctor. "Well, I'll step out a minute to let you get undressed, so I can check you over."

Ron bent over and took off his shoes and socks, and then removed his shirt and pants leaving only his underwear.

The doctor entered the room and said, "I was looking over your chart with some of my colleagues, and we all think that the biopsy was inconclusive. Which to put it matter-of-factly is that we are not in agreement with the initial findings, and would like to take a tissue sample from some other areas of your body. The spot on your shoulder appears to be healing nicely. A mole or spot like the one you had is measured by its depth into the skin and surrounding tissue. Your spot was deeper and appeared to have little strands, which were too close to being a problem than say, just a surface mole that has not had a chance to develop a deeper root. You see, these little things sprout fine little roots that will head for the nearest gland. Our bodies have these glands that help regulate different body functions. When a gland is invaded by these little strands or roots, it is there that the cancerous cells have a better chance to take hold, and expand to other places or organs throughout the body. Is that something you can understand? I am trying to explain the process in the simplest way possible, without getting too technical." He looked over at Reno and smiled.

Reno asked, "Does that mean that you want to take some more samples today?

"Yes, sir," Dr. Ingall answered.

Ron groaned and the two men looked at him.

"Well, Ron let's take a look at you," said the doctor.   Ron bent and bowed in every direction Dr. Ingall instructed him, as the examination of his entire body progressed.   The doctor drew little circles around every spot that looked to be in question.   The entire procedure took well over an hour.   During the examination, Dr. Ingall kept quiet, as did Ron, except for Ron's deep sigh every time the Doc made a new circle on his back. Most all the marks the doctor made were on his back, with a few on his thighs.   In all, there were eleven marks on Ron's body.

The doctor sat back and removed the magnifying appendage, he had attached to his glasses.   He looked at Ron and said, "I found a few spots that I didn't like, and a few we will remove, just for the sake of a future problem.   There is one on your leg that I think is going to have to be cut off, that will go deeper than any others will.   That's the one that you will find will give you the most discomfort as the next week passes.   Ron felt the blood rush to his face and sweat bead on his forehead.

"What do you mean, 'cause discomfort?" he asked the doctor.

"Well," said Dr. Ingall, "the incision will be very deep and the amount of tissue I remove will be about three inches long and two inches across. I will give you some medication for the pain, but you will have to stay off of your feet for at least a week as the wound heals.   In ten days, you can return, and I will remove the stitches, and deal with the smaller areas that are on your back and shoulders.   We should have the biopsies back by then and go from there.   Some of the spots on your back can be frozen off, so that's a good thing."

Ron was just a little comforted by that thought, but the day's worry was on his right thigh.   He sat back in the chair and let the doctor work on his leg.   While the doctor stuck needles in his leg to get the area numb, Ron thought about Grace, and the plans they had made for the upcoming weekend.   The winter weather was approaching, and the time for hiking was at its best, not too hot and not too cold. Now he would have to sit back and be patient while he mended.

Dr. Ingall said, "Gentlemen, I want you to relax for a moment while I get my assistant to come in and give us a hand." With that, the doctor rose from the stool and walked out the door.

"How you feeling?" asked Reno.

"I feel like crap," said Ron. "I have a stomachache and my head is pounding a bit. I think having to walk out of here, after this surgery, is going to make me even sicker. Just knowing I will have to be stuck on my back for a week is not making me feel good."

"Don't worry. I will be around to help you out," said Reno.

Mere moments passed before Dr. Ingall entered with his assistant, Nurse Andrea Brown. She was a petite redhead in her late forties. She had a warm calming smile. Dr. Ingall made the introductions and sat back on his stool. Ron's leg was numbed pretty well in the spot where the doc injected it with the anesthetic. Nurse Brown prepared the instruments she had removed from the cabinet. The doctor turned all his attention to preparing the area for the incision. He shaved it quickly and added more antiseptic. He suggested Ron lay back in the reclining chair and try to relax.

Ron looked at Reno who said, "I don't want to look, but it's like a train wreck. You don't want to look, but you have, too. Just lay back, son," said Reno.

"You may feel a slight burn," said Dr. Ingall, "but it is nothing to worry about. Let me know if you need more of the numbing juice."

Ron looked down at the doctor's hands and saw him cut through his skin. The incision did burn a little, but the sight of his leg being cut open was more of a psychological hurt than physical.

"How you doing, Ron?" asked the Doctor. "I can handle it," said

113

Ron. "Don't worry Doc, just get it all out.   I don't want to do this again, if I can help it."

"That's the plan.   Andrea, could you give me some more sponges, and get that little jar ready?   I am almost finished, Ron.   Okay, open up the jar," he said to Andrea, and he put the little piece of Ron's thigh into the container.   "Alright, Ron, I am going to stitch you up.   You may feel a little burn and some pulling.   Ron was lying back on the reclined chair.   He didn't want to look at what the doctor was doing.   He could feel the pulling and stretching of the flesh on his leg, as the doctor pulled the stitches into place to hold the wound closed so it would heal quickly.   The whole procedure took just a few moments, and Ron was ready for a bandage to cover the area to guard against infection.

"Well, that's it," said Dr. Ingall.   "Do you want to check it out before I cover it up?"

"Sure," said Ron, and he sat up in the chair and peered down at his leg, and studied the cut and the dark colored material that the doctor used to close it up.   Reno got up from his chair, and looked closely at the stitches and said, "Wow!   That's going be a pretty scar right there."

"It shouldn't be too, bad," said Dr. Ingall.   "I think in a couple of months you won't even notice it."

"As long as that's the worst of it," said Ron," I think I will be able to live with it."

Dr. Ingall proceeded to apply the bandages and explained as he worked that it would hurt more after the anesthetic wore off over the next few hours.   He prescribed a series of painkillers and medications to prevent infection, and suggested Ron get home and lay down with his feet elevated for the next few days without exception other than going to the bathroom.   Ron groaned as he answered the doctor with a "yes sir," and Reno agreed that he would be around to make sure Ron would be following the doctor's instructions to a tee.   As Dr. Ingall got up from his stool, he removed his latex gloves and tossed them with the pile of bloody tools and sponges that the nurse was attending.   He then turned and shook Ron and Reno's hands.

"Gentlemen, I have more work to do, but I'll be in touch once we receive the results from the biopsies.   You will need to make an appointment with the front desk for the stitches to be removed and to address the other areas I circled on your back and shoulders."

"Thanks, Doc." said Ron as Dr. Ingall closed the door behind him. Ron started to get dressed as the nurse went about her business of cleaning the exam room.   He put on his shirt and stopped.   "Excuse me Ma'am," he said in a very quiet shy way.

"Yes, sir," she answered.

"I umm…umm," Ron was stuttering for the words to come out. "I cannot put on my pants.   The nurse smiled and Reno chuckled under his breath, but it wasn't very funny to Ron.   He was in his underwear and had nothing to put on to cover up to walk out of the office."

Reno said, "I'll tie your shoes for you, but I can't help you with your pants."

"Don't worry, gentlemen, I have a solution for you.   Just wait here and I will be back in a minute."

Ron sat patiently, while Reno chuckled.   "I guess you'll have to wear a bath robe for a while.

"Yes, I have one at home, but I need to get there first."

Just then, the door opened, and the nurse came in with a clear plastic bag with clean, sanitary hospital pajama bottoms.   "Here Mr. Miller, try these.   They are not the warmest for the weather outside this time of year, but it will get you home with some dignity."   Nurse Brown took the pajamas out of the bag, and said, "Here let me help you get these on." The pajamas were split down the back and tied together in six different spots.   They were easy to get on, and didn't hurt Ron in any way.   Reno and Ron were set to go.

Reno carried Ron's pants in the plastic bag.   A wheel chair was sitting outside the door of the exam room, and once Ron sat down, Nurse Brown pushed him to the waiting room.   Here Ron and Reno waited for the receptionist to give them an appointment for the removal of the stitches and to schedule the next procedure to remove more of the questionable areas on Ron's back.

Nurse Brown came back to Ron before they left and helped him up from the chair and set him up with crutches for the rest of his rehab the following week.   As Ron and Reno headed for the exit, Nurse Brown reminded Ron to stay off his feet for the next week and not to get the stitches wet.   "Yes, Ma'am," said Ron.

"Thank you," said Reno.   "We will see you next week."   Reno helped Ron to the curb and said, "You wait here and I will go get the truck. There is no need for you to hobble across this lot."

"Thanks, Dad," said Ron.   Reno proceeded to walk across the lot to retrieve his truck.   Ron felt lucky he had his dad around to help him out.

It was late afternoon by the time Ron got settled in his bed, his leg was hurting and the painkillers were not kicking in yet.   Reno made him a sandwich and some soup, but it was not food he wanted—he just wanted to sleep.

"Thanks, Dad. I will eat this a little at a time, but I promise I will eat as much as possible. I am beat, it's been a long day," said Ron.

"Yes, I am tired, too," said Reno.

"Grace should be here in a while.   She is supposed to stop by after work.   She will take care of me, and you can probably head home soon," replied Ron.

"Well, I will stay until she gets here, if that's alright with you," he said.

"Sure, sure, that's alright. I am not trying to run you off. I'm just saying you have been a big help, and I know you are tired," Ron stated sincerely.

Reno replied, "I think I am going to sit in the recliner in the living room and take a little nap and maybe catch up on the news. Just wake me up when she gets here."

"Alright Dad," said Ron, "you go ahead and get some rest. I will have Grace wake you if you don't hear her when she comes in."

As Reno walked out of the bedroom, Ron yelled out, "Hey! Don't lock the door. She doesn't have a key, and I may be knocked out by these pills the doc gave me."

"No problem," answered Reno. "Get some rest. I'll see you later or just yell if you need anything."

"Thanks," yelled Ron.

The medication Ron had taken was also good for causing drowsiness, and that's what was starting to happen. Ron was getting sleepy and his pain was beginning to subside. As long as he kept still, he was spared the sharp sting that the stitches gave him from moving and stretching the incision. It wasn't long before the house was quiet and the two men were sound asleep.

Chapter Nineteen

Grace spent the day trying to concentrate on her job. Every time a customer came into the store, she would get confused. Every task took longer than before. It seemed like the longest day of her life. She couldn't wait to get to Ron's house and find out what happened at the doctor's office. The worry was making her sick—she couldn't even finish her lunch. Joy called late in the day to ask if there was any news from Ron. Jeremy hadn't heard from him either, and even Joy was worried for their friend.

Grace closed the store at five and not a minute later. She headed to Ron's house. As she approached the driveway, she saw Reno's truck parked in the yard next to Ron's Jeep. That was not a good sign. The hair on her neck was standing on end and sweat was beading on her upper lip. She parked her car in the road at the front of the house and walked as fast as she could up the driveway. The dogs were wagging their tails, oblivious to the predicament their master was facing. "Hey, girls," she said as she walked past giving each a light pat on the head without stopping.

She stopped at the door and gave a quiet knock, but no one answered. She knocked a little harder, and still after a few moments no one answered. She turned the knob to see if it was locked. The door pushed open and in she went.

First, she went to the living room where Reno was snoring in his recliner; the television was on, but the volume was so low it was hard for anyone to hear. Grace left him to his dreams and moved on to the master bedroom where she found Ron lying on his back with his mouth half open.

His breathing was steady and slow. He was clearly in a deep and restful sleep—something she and he had not had since the day they found out he may have cancer.   His leg was exposed, uncovered, unlike the rest of his body, which was covered in blankets, one of which was electric.   He must have been cold she thought.

She tiptoed towards the bed and looked over the man she loved.   She thought about the first time she met this man, the very moment she knew she was in love and the man that she couldn't imagine life without.   It all seemed so long ago, but in reality it was just a few months.   So much had happened in just a few months.   It hadn't even been a year since that fateful day in the school parking lot.   So much had happened since that day, but here she was wondering what tomorrow would bring.   She reached down and adjusted Ron's blanket trying not to wake him.   He barely made a sound as she turned and walked as quietly as possible, slowly closing the door behind her.

Reno was awake now, staring at the television trying to get his body to warm up enough to lift himself off the chair that hugged his worn out body for the past few hours.   Grace entered the room, sat on the love seat across from a man she hardly knew, but had heard so much about.

"Hi, Mr. Miller, did you have a good nap?" she asked.

"It was okay," he replied.

"I hope I didn't wake you," she said.

"No, no, I have been in and out since I sat down.   Is he awake?" he asked.

Grace answered, "No, sir, he is out like a light."

"Good, good," said Reno. "He was in a lot of pain.   The medication must have kicked in.   The pharmacist told me he would sleep a lot from the pink ones.   All his pill bottles are on the counter in the kitchen.   He has two for the pain, one is for at night mostly, but since he isn't driving or using heavy machinery, he can take it any time he wants to sleep.   The other two are for infection.   We don't want to get that thing infected."

"What exactly is that thing?" asked Grace.

"Oh, I'm sorry, you don't know what happened, do you?" asked Reno.

"No, sir, I just saw the bandage on his leg, but I really don't know what they did to him."

"Well," said Reno, "It was pretty bad, at least in my opinion, it was pretty bad.   They found several spots on his back and one on his leg that the doctor wanted to get at today.   He has to go back in a couple weeks for the ones on his back. The doctor thought it best to give him a break, since he was going to need to be on his back for the next seven to ten days."

"Oh Lord!" said Grace, "A whole week on his back? That's going to be a neat trick!"

"You're telling me," said Reno.

"Well, I guess I'll be heading home.   He said there's nothing more I can do here today.   When he wakes up, tell him I should be here about 9:00 a.m.   I will bring him some breakfast, so make sure you tell him not to try to do anything foolish, like make something on his own.   Tell him to just stay in the bed, and I will let myself in with my own key.   It was good to see you, Grace," he said.

Grace walked to the back door with Reno, and when he stopped in the door-way, he looked back towards the bedroom where his son lay resting. He looked at Grace, a twinkle of a tear swelled in his eye.   Grace could feel the love and fear that beat in his heart.   She reached out and held his arm before he turned to walk out the door.

Reno looked into her eyes and chuckled, "Ha, I guess you caught me. I'm not the iron-fisted hard-ass I pretend to be," he said.

"No, you're not, but you're everything Ron said you were," she said. Reno gave Grace a hug and squeezed her hard.   Grace whispered behind his ear, "Don't worry.   I will be here; I will take care of him, and I love him too."

"I know you do," he said, and I know he loves you, too. Goodnight," he said.   And Reno walked out the door.

Grace watched him walk down the sidewalk until he went around the corner and out of sight.   She locked the door and turned to walk to the counter where the four little bottles of pills sat next to the sink.   She held each one in her hand and read the contents and directions to them all.

Ron's little refrigerator was behind her; she turned and went to it and opened the door.   It was small, but Ron was happy with the fact it didn't cost him a lot to run it.   All of his medication required food or at least milk when taking them.   He had soymilk; the container was almost full, and so he had that covered for a few days.   There was a carton of eggs, and some lunchmeat, mayonnaise, and other assorted condiments were scattered throughout the little shelves.

Ron brought supper home on a nightly basis and cooked it on the grill even if was raining out.   Grace knew she was going to have to make a change for him if he was going to eat for the next week.   After all, he was not going to be able to stand at a grill and flip burgers for a while.   She sat down at the table and made a list of simple meals she could prepare for him.   She decided that most of these would not fit in his little dormitory sized refrigerator.

It had been over an hour since she first came into the house and checked on Ron.   Her impatience got the best of her.   She opened the door to his room as quietly as possible.   She tip-toed to his bed side and got down on her knees and got as close to him as possible.   She laid her arms gently on his bed and put her chin on her crossed arms; she looked at him as he breathed in and out.   She was as close as she could be without touching him and risking the chance he would awake.   She stayed in that position for a while and then lay her head down across her arms just inches away from his head and fell asleep.   Grace had burned herself out with worry throughout the day, but now she could rest.   She hadn't been asleep for long when she felt a hand brush across her head.   She looked up to see the smile that jumped her heart back to life.

"How are you feeling?" he asked her.

"That's the question I am supposed to ask you, silly. How are you feeling?"

"I am fine," he answered, "just a little sore, but I'll be back to hiking before you know it."

"I know you will," she said, "but right now, it's not what's important."

"Not important?" he asked. "What do you mean, not important? I don't know if I would be able to breathe if I couldn't get out in the woods and hike on my own. This is going to be the longest week of my life." Grace was smiling back at him as he looked back at her. "Well, maybe it won't be so bad. Come here," he said as he kissed Grace.

"Don't even think about it," she said, "you are not going to get me to fall for that one. Not tonight. I think I should get up and get you something to eat. Do you want another pain pill?" she asked. "The bottles say you need to eat something every time you take a pill."

"I see how this is going to go, Nurse Cranky. By the way, send in my girlfriend if you see her out there," he said.

"Well, I guess you haven't lost your sense of humor," said Grace.

Chapter Twenty

The days grew longer as the week rolled on. The only bright spots came when Grace would arrive from working at the music store. She made him dinner and sat with him watching television late into the night. During the day, Reno would pop in and out helping with the chores, feeding the dogs and helping Ron to get in and out of the bathtub. By Friday, Ron had had enough of being pampered and doctored. It was time for some fresh air.

Grace arrived at the same time as every other day, but this time Ron was waiting at the door. He was dressed in jogging pants and a sweatshirt. He was wearing his hiking boots and had a ball cap on his head. Grace ran up to the storm door on the back porch, but before she could reach out for the handle, Ron opened it for her. There he stood, with his jacket in hand and a grin on his face.

"If there isn't anything in here you need, then I suggest we jump in your car and go for a ride," he said.

"Well, I guess there's nothing I can think of," replied Grace. "Did you already eat supper?" she asked.

"No, I haven't," he said, "and that's why I am suggesting we just get out of here and go find something to eat. I have had enough of sitting around the house. I think I am going to go crazy if I don't see some new walls and some new scenery.

She laughed, "Well, what do you want to do? What are you in the mood for?" she asked.

"I would love to have a cold beer and some hot wings," he answered.

"Well, let's go," said Grace. She took Ron's jacket from him; he grabbed his crutches and hobbled past her towards the sidewalk. She locked the door for him and followed behind. The sun was going down and the air was growing cold.

"I may need to have that beer warmed up a bit before I drink it," said Ron. "It's getting chilly out here."

"Yep, winter is coming," said Grace. "My mom has been decorating the front of the house for Halloween all week. We always love the little kids in the neighborhood coming to the front door and getting candy. Some of them are so cute."

"We don't get trick-or-treaters here," said Ron. "All the years I have lived here, it's been quiet. I think they all go downtown to the park for the Halloween parade. Anyways, it's probably safer; the neighborhood is full of thugs that would probably rob you for a candy bar to trade for drugs."

"That's not a nice thing to say about your neighbors," said Grace as she laughed.

"Well, it's true. I'm not going to candy coat it just because I live in the middle of it. No pun intended."

Grace laughed out loud. "I think you took too many of those little pain pills," she said.

"No, no," said Ron. "I haven't had one all day, and the antibiotics are all gone, too. I have had enough of those little mind-numbing bad boys." She was laughing again.

"I may have to run back to the house if you don't stop making me laugh. I'm going to pee my pants."

Ron started laughing, too. "Alright, I'll keep quiet for a while," he said as they reached the bottom of the driveway where Grace's Camaro was parked. She held Ron's crutches as he slid into the car and onto the seat.

124

"Wow! That was a workout in itself," he said. "I need to get back to work and start working out again; this is ridiculous. Just a couple of days on my butt, and I am already out of shape."

"You're not out of shape," said Grace, "you just need to stretch out; your body is tightening up from sitting around and sleeping a lot. It's pretty normal. You will be fine in a couple of weeks after you get back to work and exercising again."

"You know I have to go through this again?" he said. "Next week the doctor is going to hack up my backside."

"I know," she answered, "let's hope you don't have too many bad spots like the one on your leg. Besides, I haven't been thinking about it too much. I have been concentrating on our trip to the Smokies in the spring. I'm trying to keep positive thoughts in my head."

Ron groaned. "I'm so sorry, Grace. If I thought this was going to happen to me, I would never have gotten involved with anyone. I don't want you to worry about me. The worst feeling in the world for me is to be a worry for someone."

"It's too late Ron. I got you in my heart, and that's not going to change now. Let's just go have some fun. It's Friday. I'm hungry, you're hungry. We can put all the worry on the back burner and just talk about the Smokies."

"What do you say we forget about this crap for the night and work on planning for the hiking trip?"

"That sounds like a good idea, I am hungry and I do have a few questions I could talk to you about. So, where do you want to go?"

"There's a new place down in the shopping center by the highway. Jeremy was bragging about it when he called a couple days ago. He said he and Joy ate there last weekend, and they thought the food was good. He said he had a dozen hot wings, and they were some of the best he had ever eaten.   And Joy had a turkey burger that was 'fat and juicy.' I think those were the exact words he used to describe it.   So I have been dreaming about wings all day, and it's been a long time since I had a cold glass of beer.   Since you're driving, I am going to have a couple.   Is that okay with you?" he asked.

"Yeah, sure," she said, "I don't think I have ever seen you drink more than a glass or two of wine, so this should be very interesting."

"Oh, no, I see where this is going.   You want to get me drunk so you can take advantage of me.   Well, let me tell you something there, young lady.   I'm just going to have a couple beers and that's that.   Besides, you don't need to pour alcohol in me.   I am all yours."   Grace laughed, but didn't say anything else for the rest of the ride to the restaurant.

The weekend went by quickly for Ron.   Grace kept him busy running him around visiting Jeremy and Joy and going to her house for dinner with her family.   Jack and Brenda met them at Zack's for lunch on Saturday. Jack had Ron laughing so hard at his pool hall jokes that tears rolled down his cheeks.   Sunday afternoon dinner was a real treat for Grace.   Her family entertained Ron, and made him feel at home.   It was a special time for Grace.   The pains of the past were far away, and the worries of tomorrow were a distant thought.   Nothing was going to get in the way of her happiness at that moment.

Chapter Twenty-One

Monday morning, sitting in the chair in the exam room, Reno continued to quiz Ron about the events of the past weekend. Reno had not met Grace's family and only met her twice in all. Ron tried to recall the rhymes and jokes that Jack had told him. The ones he got right had Reno in stitches. It was a good way to keep the tension of the moment at bay. Dr. Ingall came into the room after a while. He had a somber look on his face. Ron and Reno were quiet, waiting for the doctor to deliver his findings from the biopsy.

"Good morning, gentleman." Ron was wearing jogging shorts and his bandage was exposed front and center for the doctor to remove in his own time.

"Well," he said, "we got the results back, and it is just what we thought. The cancer got to the lymph node in your groin, but I think we got to it in time. You will have to go through chemotherapy, and we will monitor you to see if there is any change.

"What about the lump under my arm?"

"That was caused by the problems on your shoulder and back. That's what we will try to take care of today," he answered. "But first, I want to check your leg." There was a knock at the door and it opened slowly at first. It was the same nurse from last week, Andrea Brown.

"Good morning," she said, "how you doing?' she asked Ron.

"I guess I could be worse," he answered. She smiled back at him.

"Good morning, doctor," she said.

"Good morning, Nurse Brown. Could you slide the trash can over here, please?" She moved the can beside the exam table. Dr. Ingall removed the bandage from the area he had worked on the week before. He studied the stitches and the tissue that surrounded it.

"Well, it looks like you're healing just fine," he said to Ron. "I think we'll leave the stitches in for couple a more days; there's a lot of strain on the skin because of the size of the incision. Andrea, would you get some bandages to cover this?"

"Yes, sir," she answered.

"Alright Ron, why don't you take off your shirt, and we'll get started?"

It took a few hours to freeze off six moles, and surgically remove two that needed one stitch each. The procedure was not as painful as Ron had expected, but it still stung a little at times.

"I think we got everything I was worried about, and a few that I thought were good just to freeze off for good measure. I want you to come back Wednesday. I will remove the stitches and check the spots on your back. Andrea would you clean up and place bandages on these spots? Ron, do you think you will need another prescription for the pain medication?"

"No, sir, I have a few left from last week." He answered.

"Okay, you should be all set. I will see you in a couple days, and I should be able to schedule you for your chemo treatments by then."

"Thanks, Doc," said Ron.

"No problem. Do you have any questions?"

"Yes," said Reno, "I do. My wife, his mother, died from skin cancer. Is that what is causing his problems, and if it is, did you get it in time? Is he going to have a problem for life, or is this a one-time deal?"

"Well, I think we can take care of it with treatment. Whether or not it is a one-time deal is hard to answer. I think," he said as he was looking at Ron, "you will have to get a checkup every year for the rest of your life, and maybe every six months for a few years. I am hopeful that after these treatments you will be cancer free and will stay cancer free for as long as we can stay ahead of any potential problems. That's all I can say for now until we get further into the treatment process. I can only make a guess at what will or will not turn up next. Let's just stay hopeful and positive. I have found that attitude is a major factor in a person's health and prognosis."

"Thanks again, Doc," said Ron.

"Mr. Miller, is there anything else, or any other questions?"

"No, Doc. I guess I know all there is to know. Thank you for all your help. I'm sure you'll do everything you can to keep my boy around."

"That's the plan," said Dr. Ingall. "Now, if you will excuse me, I have few more patients to see." The doctor was gone and Ron, Reno and the nurse were left in the quiet little exam room.

Ron's shoulders were a little sore and certain movements he made stung a little. Grace stopped by after work and he explained everything the doctor had said during his visit. She wasn't comforted by his calm confident attitude. As far as Ron was concerned the subject was closed, and talking about it wasn't going to make it any better. She gave in to his wish and let it go. They would not discuss it any more for the time being.

Chapter Twenty-Two

The treatments started a week after the stitches were removed. At first, he didn't seem to be affected by the chemicals he was swallowing. But by the third treatment, he was sick all of the time and losing his hair. Working as a sheriff's deputy required that he kept it cut short, so shaving it all off was not much of a hardship. Most people didn't even know he was going through the treatments. He took vacation time and a medical leave for the duration of the surgery. He worked as much as possible and pushed himself through the training hikes he took with Grace on the weekends.

Halloween came and went with Ron at home sick and Grace nursing him through the bitter vomiting and stomach pain. All she could do was keep him hydrated with ice cold water and massage his forehead to help him sleep. Her rides home alone in the evening were filled with tears. Her heart was breaking. Once again, she felt she had no control like someone was holding her down and smothering the life out of her. Her mom was there every night to hold her and soothe her aching heart.

In between the treatments were good times again. The days would get better until the next treatment, and then it would start again—the roller coaster ride from ill to feeling better for weeks on end. The hike in the spring rarely got mentioned, as if it was just a dream that was pushed aside, like so many dreams that people have that they eventually give up on. Grace was looking forward to the day when the treatments were over.

Monday morning, like clockwork Reno arrived for the trip to the cancer treatment center. Ron was watching out the window for him. "Good morning Pop," said Ron.

"Good morning, son," said Reno. "Are you ready for another fun day at the hospital?"

"No, Pop, I'm not. I am tired of being tired and sick of being sick. Poor Grace is a wreck. I know this is killing her, too." Ron's eyes swelled with tears. As they rolled down his cheeks, he tried to clear his throat. "I want to do so many things with her. I can't even get out of the bed on most days to take a bath. She's been so good pretending to be strong, but I know she cries a lot." He tried to clear his throat again.

There was a silent pause for a moment before Reno said, "I remember when your momma went through this mess. It was tough for her, too. I couldn't help her any more than I can help you."

"Dad, I couldn't do this without you. The only things that keep me from giving up are you and Grace. I want so much to make her happy."

"Hey, you're going to be alright! You've got what…thirteen or fourteen more trips to this place? It will be over before you know it, and the weather will be turning warmer by then. You just have to hang in there a little while longer."

"Let's change the subject," said Ron. "Maybe if we talk about something else, I won't think about tonight, when I'm leaning into the toilet bowl puking my guts out."

"Good idea," said Reno. "Let's not think about toilets and puking. What have you got planned for Thanksgiving?

"Grace and I are going to Joy and Jeremy's house. What are you doing?" he asked Reno.

"I think Emily and I are going to have dinner at her church. Her daughter is going to be vacationing down in Florida. Her church puts on a Thanksgiving Day meal for the members; and some of the homeless people from the shelter get bused-in, and they feed a bunch of them. We figured it would be fun to help with that."

"Wow, that's pretty cool," said Ron.

"Yes, well it's the least I can do; she's been pretty good to me. Besides, I have to be a 'good boy,' if want to get the goodies that come after dessert, if you know what I mean." Ron laughed so hard his belly hurt. He laughed off and on until the ride home, when his stomach turned upside down again from the chemo. Reno had put a little sunshine on Ron's dreary Monday morning.

The weeks went by and as Thanksgiving approached, Ron wondered if he would be able to keep his turkey dinner down or if it was a mistake to think he would be well enough to enjoy the day. Mondays were the worst and into Tuesday. By Thursday, he was usually feeling better, but sometimes it was difficult. Thanksgiving morning Grace came by early to help him get dressed.

"Ron, do you want to wear a tie? I see you have a couple of them in your closet."

"No," he answered. "I usually get gravy all over them. I save them for weddings, funerals and courtrooms."

"Weddings? I don't think I have ever heard that word come out of your mouth before." Ron was in the bathroom, his face partially covered in shaving cream and he was staring in the mirror, when the words she just said were processed in his mind. He watched as a tear formed in his eye. He looked deep inside himself. The silence was deafening. Grace yelled back again. "Did I say something wrong?" With the cream still on his face, Ron put the razor down and walked from the bathroom towards Grace.

She was still pushing clothes back and forth on the rack in his closet. She turned to see him walking towards her; he was staring at her with a half-smile on his face.

"What's wrong?"

"Nothing," he said, and he got down on one knee in his bedroom, with a face full of shaving cream and a tear rolling down his cheek looking up at her from the floor, he said, "Grace, I love you with all my heart. My life has been made complete since you came into it. I have never felt like this before. Grace, I want you to be my wife. Will you marry me?"

Grace was overwhelmed. Her heart was pounding. Even before he asked the question, just seeing him on his knee she knew what he was going to say. "Yes, Ron! Oh, yes! I will marry you and be the happiest woman on earth!"

"I don't have a ring for you, but we can find one sometime before the holidays are over."

"I don't care about that," she said. "Get up and kiss me," she said. She helped him back to his feet and gently wiped most of the cream from his face exposing his lips. She kissed him tenderly trying not to get any of the cream on her own face. She giggled as their lips met. "I love you too," she said. She pulled back away from him and stared into his eyes.

He asked, "What do we do now?" He was confused; he didn't expect to be engaged today, and now he was lost.

Grace smiled at him and said, "You go finish shaving. I will keep trying to find something you can wear that matches my dress."

"We're going to be alright, aren't we?"

"Yes," she whispered. "Yes, we're going to be just fine."

He shook his head and turned back towards the bathroom to finish shaving. It was a hard thing to do with a smile he couldn't wipe off his face, no matter how hard he tried.

Chapter Twenty-three

When Ron and Grace arrived at Jeremy and Joy's, they were both lightheaded with happiness. Jeremy knew something was up when Ron couldn't stop smiling.

"I guess you're feeling good today," said Jeremy.

"Oh, yes, it's a good day. It's Thanksgiving, right?"

"Yes, it's Thanksgiving," said Jeremy as he squinted at Ron. "What's going on? I've known you for years, and I know that something is going on."

"Not a thing," said Ron. "Not a thing. It's Thanksgiving, right?"

"Yes, you already said that."

"Hey, where's Joy? I want to give my old girl a hug."

"She's in the kitchen doing what she does best. You go on in and say hello. I will be right here on the swing waiting for you because I think something is going on."

Ron almost skipped through the house to get to the kitchen to where Grace was helping Joy with the mixing of side dishes. He looked at Grace while he hugged Joy and smiled. He knew she was keeping their secret. They had made a pact on the way to the house not to spill the beans until they were all sitting at the table so they could make a toast and ask them to be the Best Man and Matron of Honor.

Joy gasped for air and squeezed back. "I missed you! Jeremy says you've been feeling bad." She let him go and looked him over. "You look pretty good. How do you feel today?"

"Well," he said, "I hope I can keep the turkey down. I feel pretty good, a little queasy, but it gets better by the weekend, until Monday when I go back again. Then I have a couple of bad days. I only have a few more treatments and then more tests. And then, well, I just have to wait and see. But as the doc says, 'a positive yet realistic attitude is the best medicine,' so I am trying to stay true to form and maintain an optimistic outlook. After all, we have to hike up to Clingman's Dome in the spring."

"Yes, you're right," said Joy, "that is good medicine, and I am glad you brought up the trip because I want to start planning for it. I think today would be a chance to get the ball rolling. We could make a list of things we need to take, where we are going to sleep and what we will be eating."

"Actually, Miss Joy, Grace and I have already made a list, and I have planned the whole thing, right down to the place where you will be able to use a bathroom for the last time," said Ron.

"What? The last time I can use a bathroom?"

"Well, yes, you didn't think there were toilets in the middle of the Smoky Mountains for dainty little girls like you, did you?"

"Oh, I think you're feeling just fine," she said. Joy looked at Grace, who was smiling from ear- to-ear, and turned to push Ron from the kitchen.

"Okay now. You can leave and go play with the big boys while us 'dainty little girls' get the turkey ready. Ron held his ground for a second but relented to her fervent motion. He laughed like a little child getting the leftover frosting bowl from a cake his mother just finished icing.

"Go on, get out of here, you little brat."

She looked at Grace and said, "I was hoping you were going to be able to straighten that man out, but I think you made him worse."

"Oh, come on," said Grace, "Give him a break. I don't think he had laughed like that since this whole thing started. So, maybe it's a good thing. Besides, he loves you two so much. I think he considers you to be as much family as I do my own flesh and blood family. Who, by the way, we have to visit later to have dessert. I hope I can save room because I am going to dig into that sweet potato pie like it was the last one on earth."

The girls set the table and finished cooking the side-dishes, while Ron and Jeremy sat on the porch and talked about the cases they were working on at the sheriff's department.

"It sure is a pretty day," said Ron.

"Yes, it is. We are truly blessed. The weather reports were calling for cloudy and cool, but I guess it's going to hold off until this afternoon. So, buddy what's up? I know you got something going on you're not telling me," said Jeremy.

"What are you talking about?" asked Ron. "I don't have any secrets from you."

"Now buddy," said Jeremy, "we have been friends for a good many years, and I know when you have something on your mind."

"Jeremy, I think you are being paranoid. It is out of character for you. What do you think is going on?"

"I don't know, but I will figure it out!"

Just then, the door opened, and Grace came out to announce that the table was set, and the bird was ready for carving.

"Joy said you're doing the carving, Jeremy, and she said for me to tell you it is ready, and you need to get your butt in here and get to work."

"I got it," he said, and walked by her through the door into the house. Ron walked behind him, but Grace stopped him in the doorway.

"You didn't say anything to him, did you?"

"No," he replied.   "But I think he knows something is up.   He just doesn't know what yet, but if we give him enough time, I will bet he guesses."   Ron reached for her, and they kissed in the doorway.   From the dining room, they could hear Joy calling for them to hurry and come in before everything got cold.   The four of them sat at the table.

"Jeremy, would you like to say a prayer and bless the day?"

"Sure," he said. "It would be an honor. 'Lord, we give thanks for the food we are about to receive, for the blessings that being alive bring, and for the presence of our dearest friends Grace and Ron, and for giving me the love of this most wonderful woman. Amen."

"That was beautiful," said Grace.

"You're a lucky lady, Joy," said Ron.

"No, I am a lucky man," said Jeremy.

"I think you are full of crap," said a teary eyed Joy.   "Now someone pass me those potatoes please!"

The meal was special for all the right reasons—good company, good food, and good weather.   When it was over and the dishes were cleared, the group headed to their favorite place, the swing on the front porch. The rut was in full season and the deer that grazed peacefully along the tree line during the summer months were now sparring for the affections of the jittery does that were keeping their distance from the amorous bucks.

"This is my favorite spot in the world," said Joy, sitting on the swing with a crocheted blanket wrapped around her and Jeremy, who was sitting next to her holding her hand under the blanket.   The swing moved back and forth slowly, comforting them both with a relaxing rhythm that a baby enjoys when in its mother arms as it is rocked to sleep.

Grace was looking to Ron to make the announcement.   He was holding back, and it was starting to make her nervous.

"Ron, I was wondering what it was you were talking about, on the way over here this morning," she asked. "You remember, don't you?"

He looked at her and smiled; he knew what she meant, but he was still shy, and that was one of the things she loved about him. It was that little boy in him that made him what he was.

"I, um, have some news I thought I might share with you two," he said looking at Jeremy and Joy. The swing stopped and the two of them looked at him as he spoke.

"Now, Jeremy, you were bugging me about holding something inside earlier, and well, I guess you were right. Maybe you should go for the detective's badge next time around."

Jeremy smirked, "Yes, I knew there was something going on with you."

"Yes there is. I was wondering; would you like to make a guess?"

Joy's eyes turned to Grace, who was fixed on every word that came from Ron's mouth.

"I think I can guess," said Joy. She turned and looked at Ron, "Have you set a date?"

"Set a date, for what?"

"Yes, I thought, so," said Jeremy, "You are getting hitched!"

Grace couldn't stand it anymore, "Yes!" she yelled, "We are going to get married!"

"When? When?" asked Joy.

And that's when Grace turned to Ron. "I don't know, Ron, when are we getting married?"

He looked back at her and said, "I hadn't actually thought about when.

I guess whenever you get out of school.   And we still have to tell your Mom and Dad.   I think they might have something to say about the 'when' part."

Grace smiled and nodded her head yes "I guess you're right; my daddy will probably have an opinion."

"Wow, you guys are really getting married!" exclaimed Joy.   "I am so happy for you!"   Joy rose from the swing and gave Grace a big hug. "Welcome to the family!" she said.

Chapter Twenty- four

Thanksgiving and the weekend that followed was one to remember. With the blessing of all who mattered, the marriage of Ron and Grace was going forward without a hitch; no date had been set and the ring was not yet picked, but with all the focus on Ron's health, it was of little consequence. With the treatments half over, Christmas was on the minds of the newly engaged couple.

Sharing the holidays with someone like Grace was something Ron could only dream of in the past. In the years before, he found himself working on Christmas and New Year's Eve to give his married colleagues the time to spend with their families. This Christmas was going to be different. Now it was his turn to celebrate the day.

"Don't forget," said Grace, "momma likes to have breakfast at 8:00 a.m., so we can start to open presents by 10:00. Then we're going to meet up with Jack and Brenda and give them their gifts."

"Don't worry," he said, "I'll be on time, but I would like to stop by my dad's and see him for a little while tomorrow."

"I think we will have plenty of time to see him," replied Grace, "and even call Joy to see if they want to get together for a little bit before we go to your house and exchange gifts."

"I thought we were exchanging gifts at your Mom's."

"That's not what I was talking about," she said.

"Oh, I see. Well, let's hope we get home early," said Ron. "I am looking forward to opening my presents." Grace giggled and kissed and hugged him goodnight. He walked her to the car, and watched as she drove away.

The weeks went by fast and the holidays came and went. The day that Grace was dreading drew near. That cold February day, that changed the destinies of so many was not going to be celebrated, but remembered for what it was; a turning point around which the future would evolve, and people transformed from lost to found. From that day on, the eyes would see more and the heart would hold on to the beat of the world.

The cancer treatments nearly put a halt to the training hikes and workouts at the Graham Recreation Center. Grace spent most of her spare time caring for Ron. Classes started and working at the music store left her little time for anything else. It was a roller coaster ride trying to keep him healthy; his weight had dropped and his energy was sapped. The weekends were the best times. The treatments were on Mondays, and by Saturday and Sunday, he was just starting to feel like himself, and then he had to turn around the next day and go through it all over again. The spring hike was put on hold. There was no way he would be in shape to climb a mountain like that of Clingman's Dome.

Winter was cold and dragged on slowly making it seem worse than it truly was. When April finally came, no one was more elated than Ron and Grace. The final treatment came a week before Easter Sunday. It was a tough long process, but all the tests showed that Ron was free of the cancer that had threatened to end his life. It was time to get back to living.

As the weeks passed, the sun climbed higher into the sky and the days grew longer. Leaves were popping from the tips of branches that reached out for the summer sun. The training for the springtime hike now turned to training for a hike in the fall. Labor Day weekend signified the end of summer and the start of another semester of school for Grace.

"Ron, do you think we will need new fuel containers? I think mine is getting low. How about yours; is it feeling light? We did cook a lot of meals on the practice hikes."

141

"Yes, we did," he answered. "We should probably start out with new fuel containers; even the lighters should be replaced. I actually made a list of things we should get to replace the stuff we used all summer."

"Definitely batteries," she said. "My headlamp is weak. Even my sock liners are a little worn out. Do you think we could go shopping for some clothes? I really want to get a new pair of pants."

"Sure, I was planning on getting a couple pairs of socks myself. What kind of pants were you thinking about getting?"

"There's a few on sale at the hiking store in Durham that I wanted to check out. You can unzip the legs off and make them into shorts and then when it gets cold in the evening, you can zip them back on."

"That's something I could check out for myself," he said. "We only have a few days left, so I guess we should go tomorrow night after I get off duty. Is that good for you? What time are you getting off from the music store?"

"I leave at 5:00 p.m. after the night girl comes in. She is usually a little late. She has to drop off her son at the babysitters, but after she gets there, I will come right over and pick you up. We can get something to eat before we hit the stores."

"That sounds like a good plan," he said.

Labor Day weekend finally arrived. After training for months to get into shape to climb the steep slopes up to Clingmans Dome, the gang of four was on their way. Traveling through Maggie Valley and seeing the towering peaks out in the distance brought shivering goose bumps. The excitement was only tempered by the storm clouds that were filling the skies to the south. The weather reports stated a severe late summer thunderstorm would be passing through the area before the day would end.

"I hope we get to the campground before that storm hits," said Grace. "I don't want to set up the tent in a down pour."

"I hope it doesn't rain, at all," said Jeremy. "We don't have as good a tent as you do.   I got mine at the discount store.   It works well, but if we get a down pour, I am afraid we will get wet."

"I think it will be fun," said Joy. "Where is that adventurous spirit?"

"We should stay positive and think good dry thoughts," said Ron. Jeremy started to chant, "No rain--no rain."   Grace chimed in along with him. "No rain, no rain," they chanted louder.   Ron got a few shouts in before they all started to laugh.

The campground was beautiful, surrounded by steep mountain slopes. Just at the foot of the Smoky Mountain National Park, a fast moving crystal clear mountain creek split the campground in half.   As they crossed the bridge to get to their sites, Ron slowed the Jeep down and peered down into the water.

"Look!" he yelled, "Can you see those fish?   I think those are native brook trout. I wish I had brought my fishing pole.   Darn!   It would have been nice to eat some fresh cold water trout for supper tonight."

"I don't think so," said Joy, "Besides, I brought a nice steak to cook on the grill."

"I wouldn't mind trying some brook trout," said Jeremy.   "Maybe next time we come up this way, we can remember to bring a pole."

"I had trout before.   I didn't think it was bad. My dad caught some on a camping trip we went on some years ago.   I can't even remember where we went, but I remember him cooking them in a frying pan with butter, and he rolled them in flour after dipping them in evaporated milk. I thought they tasted a lot better than the squirrels he made us try once when he got back from a hunting trip."

Jeremy laughed out loud, "Your Dad made you eat squirrel, too?

"When I was a kid, my dad used to make me eat all kinds of wild game. You know my mom passed when I was young, so I didn't have anyone to protect me from his gourmet recipes." They all laughed.

"I am going to pee my pants, if you don't stop soon. I need to go to the ladies room," said Joy.

Ron drove up to a small block building in the middle of the park. "Here you go," he said. Joy got out. "Hey, we are going to park at the site; it's only about a hundred feet or so from here. Are you okay walking over, or do you want us to wait for you?"

"No, you all go ahead; it looks like the rain is coming, so I'll be fine."

"Alright, see you there," he said.

They parked the Jeep at the camp site and proceeded to get the tents set up before the skies opened up with the rain.

"Grace, grab the tent stakes, and I'll lay the tarp down and lay out the tent."

Grace proceeded to stick the stakes in the ground through the little eye hooks, Ron stretched the tent out and hooked the poles into the clips. Once the tent fly was attached, they ran back and forth to the Jeep tossing their sleeping bags and bed pads into the two-man tent that had been Ron's for years. Grace put a change of clothes and some night slippers into the little tent.

Jeremy, on the other hand, had a four man tent with a small rain fly that barely covered the top of the dome. He was having problems setting it up as quickly as he would like. He started to curse under his breath. He was running back-and-forth from side-to-side, reading and rereading the directions, trying to figure out how to get his shelter up and his gear into it before the impending storm reached the little valley that they were calling home for the night.

"Hey, did you know there are no showers in there?" asked Joy. "I thought I could at least be clean for this little expedition."

"I said I would make sure you had a potty nearby. I never said anything about a hot shower and a blow dryer," replied Ron, as he laughed at the angry stare she was sending in his direction.

"Hey, honey," said Jeremy, "If we don't get this tent up, I am going to bet that you get your wish for a shower, but it is not going to be the one you want."

She looked up into the southern sky in time to see a bolt of lightning race across a blackened sea of howling wind blown rain. "Rain, oh my gosh," she said out loud.

Ron ran and closed the windows and doors to the Jeep. Grace and Joy feverishly joined Jeremy to get the tent set and the fly on to help keep the rain out.

"I hope this storm passes quickly," said Joy as she ran back-and-forth attaching the stakes to the lines. As quickly as possible, they jumped into their assembled shelters and hunkered down to ride out the storm. The tents were set about twenty feet apart, but they had no problem hearing each other laughing through the thunder and relentless downpour. It rained hard for over an hour.

Grace was warm, snuggled up to Ron in their dry tent with the rain fly that went down to the ground. Joy and Jeremy, on the other hand, were sitting in small puddles of rain water that had seeped through the seams of the exposed sides of the little dome tent. As the storm passed and the booms of thunder waned in the distance, the four campers poked their heads out of their tents looking like little groundhogs checking to see if the coast was clear. The creek came up several feet, and the little fish that Ron had seen when they arrived were no longer visible in the silt filled, fast-moving creek. Some tree limbs and leaves were scattered around the park, but it was minor.

"Well, that was fun," said Ron. "Everything looks to have survived," he said out loud.

Jeremy said, "I think we may need to use a towel or two.   We seemed to have sprung a leak.   We kind of took in a little water in here."

Ron looked inside the dome tent and chuckled, "I will bet you buy a better tent before you try this again, he-he, old buddy?"

"Well, at least we didn't float away," said Joy.

"I don't know,' said Jeremy.   "I kind of like this little tent.   I think we might just keep it forever."

The rain held off for the rest of the night and cool air filtered down from the mountain tops.   All night the sounds of nature filled the camp. Crickets and cicadas sang their love songs to each other until the cold air chased them down into their shelters to sleep until the sun returned and warmed their bodies back to life.   A pair of foxes barked to each other along the tree line hunting rabbits for their hungry pups hiding in the woods.   The screeches they made were haunting and Grace found it hard to believe that foxes could sound so eerie.

As morning came, the sun peaked over the tops of the mountains through the mist and fog.   Grace was warm against Ron's body.

"Good morning," he said when he woke from her arm poking him in the side.

"Good morning, to you," she said.

"Did you sleep, okay?"

"I haven't slept like this in a long time.   It was nice."   He kissed her on the forehead.   "I have to pee," he said.   "I am going to have to get up and go to the bath house.   You know… the one without a shower."

"Yes, I know the one you mean.   May I go with you?" she asked.

"Mmmmmm, I insist that you come with me."

"Oh Ron, I love it when you talk dirty to me," she teased. "You have come so far out of your shell; it is amazing the transformation!"

"Well, I have had a good teacher." They both laughed and poked at each other on the way to the bath house.

Jeremy and Joy were already awake and walking around the campground, checking out the scenery and looking at the little fish from the bridge. The creek came down a little compared to after the deluge, and the water was clear again, so the little trout were easy to see. It was a beautiful morning, perfect for hiking up a mountain.

Breakfast of champions is what Ron called it—oatmeal, blueberry bagels and cream cheese, with a lot of coffee. Joy preferred a more traditional breakfast of bacon and eggs with lots of coffee. The men cleared and packed all the gear as the ladies cooked and boiled water for the meal. The whole process was quick, which is what Ron wanted. He wanted to get on the trail as early as possible. The trail head was still an hour's drive up the mountain, and an all day hike was ahead of them from there.

When they arrived at Newfound Gap, there were already several cars, buses and travel campers scattered around the parking lot. The Appalachian Trail crossed the road and climbed back up the southern side of the Smokey Mountain National Park. The girls headed for the bathroom, the last place on the trail that they were going to be able to flush a toilet. Ron and Jeremy set out the backpacks and double checked their gear list, to make sure there was nothing missing. The girls were ready and the day was about to begin. They loaded their backpacks and locked the Jeep.

"Well," said Ron, "there's no turning back now. Let's do it!" He led them across the road to the head of the trail. He looked at Grace and smiled. "Have I told you lately that I love you?"

"Well, not for a few days at least.   Why do you ask?"

"Check this out, I found a rock back at the campground near our tent. It was fairly shiny and I thought, hey, I bet Grace would like this as little souvenir of our first big hike together.   Would you like to see it?"

"Okay, wise guy, let's see your little rock," answered Grace.

Ron dug deep into his pocket and came up with nothing.   "Oh, wait. I thought I put it in there.   Wait, maybe it's in this one, and he dug deep into his other pocket, and came out with an object that he kept hidden in his hand.   He got up close to her, and took her by the hand.   Looking deeply into each other's eyes, he put the little stone into her hand.   She looked down to see a ring of gold with a diamond.

"Oh, my God!   You know you didn't have to do this!"

"I know I didn't, but I wanted to!" he said.

Joy and Jeremy were watching as the scene played out.   Joy's eyes were filling with tears as were Grace's.

"I promise. I will never forget this hike," said Grace.   "Have I told you lately that I love you?"

"Not for a few days, at least," said Ron.

"Okay, this is getting pretty mushy," said Jeremy, "and besides you're making me look bad."   Joy socked him in the gut and said, "Be quiet, you old fart.   You were romantic, once."

"Yes, but that was a long time ago," he stated, as he caught his breath.

Grace gave Ron a kiss and looked into his eyes. "Let's do this!"

"Lead on Miss Grace," said Ron.   "The trail is lined with trees with white paint marks on them, so it is impossible to get lost."

Grace stepped off the road and onto the trail.   The bright light from the sun soon disappeared as they walked deeper into the woods.   The trail was flat for the first few hundred feet, but the terrain changed as they rounded the first corner.   Grace was leading the way, yet she turned to look back at Ron and asked, "Is this the beginning of things to come?"

Ron replied, "I hiked on the other side of Newfound Gap, but this is the first time I have ever been on this side.   We can stop for breaks any time you want.   The other side of the gap is steep and the terrain on either side of the trail is just as thick and dark as on this side, so I am going to bet we have a lot of uphill hiking for the most of the nine miles to the summit of Clingman's Dome."

Ron looked at Jeremy who was not smiling anymore.   "Are you going to be okay buddy?   I know you didn't train as much as we did."

"I should be okay as long as we take our time and eat as much of this food as soon as possible to take some of the weight out of my pack.   This thing seems to have gotten heavier since I slung it over my shoulders at the campground this morning," Jeremy replied.

Ron laughed at him and said, "Well it gets worse as the day goes on. Every little thing that we put in the bag seems to get bigger and heavier as the day goes on."

"Joy, did you add anything to this bag when I was not looking," asked Jeremy.

"No sweetie, I did not!   My pack is feeling a little heavier than when we started too.   Grace, is your bag feeling heavier?"

"Yes, and we haven't even been out here for twenty minutes," she said as she looked at her watch.

"I think we are going to have a long day."

She looked at Ron and said, "I think we will be alright. I am looking forward to seeing some new scenery."

They headed back up the trail with Grace leading the way.

Each step she took seemed to take her away from the past and further into her future with Ron. He was healthy again, and she was deeply in love with him. The trail was wet and muddy from the heavy rain the day before. Green moss covered everything that lay on the ground on the trail; the rocks that she stepped over were slick and slippery making it hard to walk without the fear of losing the battle to keep her balance. The thick canopy of trees keep the sunlight from reaching the ground, and the steep mountainside was covered with fallen trees as far as the eye could see. Everywhere she looked, the prehistoric rainforest was green with moss. It was like a carpet of emerald that stretched on forever.

"I would hate to get lost in here," she said out loud. "It is so thick it would be impossible to get through without killing yourself, but it sure is beautiful."

The members of this small group were each straining and breathing heavily as they slowly made their way towards the summit. As the trail leveled out into a small sun lit clearing, they came upon two elderly men sitting on fallen trees. The clearing was an intersection for a trail that led to a campground a few miles into a valley below the summit.

"Good morning," said the men as the group entered the rest area.

"Good morning," replied Ron as he turned to Jeremy and Joy and said, "I think this is a good place to rest for a while."

"Oh, thank God," said Jeremy. "I am already beat."

Grace was not going to argue. She slid her pack to the ground and propped it against a fallen tree. She opened it and took out a bag of cheese crackers. Joy and Jeremy ate snacks from their packs as well.

"Where are ya'll heading?" asked one of the older men.

"We are going to Clingmans Dome, but we are staying at Double Spring Gap Shelter for the night," replied Ron.   We are just out for the weekend.

"How about ya'll?"   "Are you going to the summit or heading the other way? Ron asked.

"We are going to Clingmans Dome too.   We stayed at the campground last night, but we are getting a ride back there after we get to the summit.   We made this hike twenty years ago, but it seems like it got further since then."

Ron laughed and looked at Grace.   He thought about the future for a second.   Would he be able to hike this trail again twenty years from now? Grace was thinking the same thing as she listened to the men talk.   The trail was rugged and steep and definitely not easy to hike.   She was impressed that these older men were here to begin with.

"Have you ever seen any bears out here?" Joy asked.

The two men looked at each other as they answered in unison, "No, not up here, but we did see one at the campground a few days ago.   They are up here.   We see signs all over the place."

"What do mean signs," asked Joy.

"Well, besides the tracks and the bear poop on the trails, you can see they are eating the grubs in the fallen trees since the trees are ripped apart," answered one of the older men.

"Oh, we passed a lot of fallen trees that were obviously messed up, so bears did that?" said Joy as she looked toward Jeremy.

"I do not think we need to worry, honey.   If there are any bears up here, they would surely have run off when they heard us coming."

"That's true, Miss.   Bears will run the other way as soon as they see or hear people coming," one of the gentlemen offered.

"Well, just the thought of a bear being up here gives me the shivers," said Joy.

"You should be more concerned about the pigs that roam around up here than the bears. Pigs are far more common than bears. They are tearing up the other side of the park more so than this side. This side of New Found Gap is not as bad because of the difficult terrain and the lack of food sources, but the further you go towards Fontana Lake, the more likely you will see the signs," explained the old man.

"Wild pigs," said Grace. Who would have thought that wild pigs were up here?"

"Well, I would not get too worried about bears or pigs on this trip," said Ron. "We probably will not be lucky enough to see any."

"I would not mind seeing some of those pigs," said Jeremy. "That would be a good story to tell back home.

"This end of the park is a rainforest compared to the north end," said one of the old men.

Ron rose to his feet and stretched his body, "I think we have been sitting too long he said. "Come on Grace, it's time we got moving again."

The four of them put their backpacks back together and slung them over their shoulders. Grace turned to the two older men, but they were not moving.

"We will rest a little longer," said one of the men.

"Hopefully we will see you at the top," said Grace.

"We will make it sooner or later," said the man.

"Good luck," said Joy as they headed back up the trail.

The further up they went, the steeper the trail got until it seemed as though it was a staircase that never ended. Each step got harder than the previous one. Grace and Ron were in better shape than Jeremy. They had trained on the trails at Cedar Rock Park on a daily basis and built up their endurance, but this was far more extreme. Jeremy stopped nearly every chance he could to catch his breath. Joy had walked the track at City Park after work most every night, so she was ready. Jeremy was lagging behind.

"Come on Jeremy," yelled Joy. "You can do it." He was huffing and panting, sweat was running down his face and his hair was soaked. His shirt was wet from the moisture running down his neck.

"This is hard," he barked through his labored breaths.

"Yes it is," she replied. Grace stopped on the trail. She was just out of sight of Jeremy and Joy. She set her pack down and waited for Ron to catch up. The trail turned from corner to corner as it led straight up, winding its way through the fallen trees and enormous moss-covered rocks.

"We need to slow down," Grace said to Ron as he slid his pack off next to hers.

"Yep!" he replied. "This is a rough one, and I cannot say for sure if it gets easier or harder. Let's just wait here and take a break."

It had been several hours since the couples left the flat road at New Found Gap, and they had only traveled three of the roughly nine miles they had to hike to get to the summit.

"You know," said Ron "we have to hike three miles to get to the shelter after we get to the summit."

Grace smiled and said. "Oh Lord, don't tell Jeremy that until we leave the summit. I don't think he wants to hear that.

"Yep, this may be more than we bargained for," said Ron.

Jeremy slowly made his way to the resting spot and dropped his pack to the ground.

"This is crazy," he said out loud. "This is what you call fun? This is hard work! I do not work this hard at home when I go to work. Whose idea was this?"

Everybody looked at Grace.

"This is not my fault. I recall telling you to get into shape," she said with a smile.

"Do not worry. We have all day and nothing else to do but go one step at a time. We can stop whenever we need and rest," said Ron.

After a brief rest and a long drink of water, they all strapped the packs back on and pushed on up "the stair case to hell" as Jeremy called it. Most of the time the trail was dark and closed in by the dense canopy of trees, but once in a while the sky would appear and the light would pour in. Those were the places they would stop and look out over the valley below. They hiked on the Tennessee side of the park. The sun that was above them at noon was now in the west as they drudged up the mountainside.

"Come on!" yelled Grace from up the hill high above Jeremy. "We are almost there. I can see the look out on top of the summit."

Clingman's Dome was in sight, but the hike to it was far from over. Grace was excited since she had been looking forward to this day for a long time. She had spent so many days in the woods and so many nights camping in the park practicing with her equipment while getting closer to Ron. She pushed on, not stopping to give Jeremy a rest; he would have to rest when they got to the summit. She was determined to get there and she was not going to stop again if she did not have to.

The terrain began to change as they got closer to the summit. What was damp and mossy down below was now drier. The trees were thinner now than before, and they were not as dense as the conifers down below. The group had climbed staircases of rocks up to this point, but now the trail was leveling out and even sloping a bit down before heading back up to another flat spot. Every time the trail leveled out and then down, Grace's pace would quicken, but the muscles that hurt going up were different from the muscles that hurt going down.

Grace pushed herself past the fatigue; her body screamed out for a break, but she would have none of it. Ron, though not far behind, was just as tired as she was as he struggled to keep up with her. Grace was setting a pace only she could meet. Joy and Jeremy, who were way behind Grace, did not look back. Surprisingly, they met a group of teenagers coming down the trail from the summit. Grace was startled at first as the teenagers stepped aside to let her go by. Ron stopped for a moment when he reached the kids.

"Hey!" he said, trying to catch his breath before continuing to speak, "Did you come from the summit?"

"Yes sir." said one of the older boys.

"Is it much further?" asked Ron.

"No sir." said the boy. "It's about fifteen minutes up the trail."

"Fifteen minutes!" said Ron. "Oh, that's good." Ron took off his pack and sat on a rock. "I need a break," he said to the kids.

"Where you kids headed?" he asked.

"We wanted to see what a shelter looks like," said one of the teenage girls.

"You are going all the way to Mt. Collins Shelter?" asked Ron.

"Yes sir," said the older boy.

"Do you know how far the shelter is from here?" asked Ron.

"No sir," answered the boy.

"It's about four miles down the trail," he offered

"Four miles?" said the girl.

"Yes," said Ron.

She looked at her friends in the group. "We did not know it was that far," she said as she looked at the older boy. "Terry I do not want to go that far," she said.

"It would be dark before you got back," said Ron.

The kids all thought it over and decided it was a good idea to go back up to the summit. Ron waited for Jeremy and Joy to catch up. Grace was far ahead of the group now. She could see the look-out up ahead. It was just a few minutes away. She lifted her tired aching legs over the last fallen tree that lay across the trail. She walked into a clearing that was just below the look-out. Exhausted, she dropped her backpack to the ground and sat down.

"I made it," she said between breaths. "I made it." She looked back to the trail waiting for Ron to appear. First the teenagers came into the clearing; they were talking to each other as they went past her and walked through the clearing towards the Dome.

Grace lay back against her pack; she was so happy. Joy came into the clearing first with a red faced Jeremy following behind. Ron was not in sight. Joy dropped her pack next to Grace and sat down. Jeremy just dropped to the ground and slid his pack off and took a long drink from his water. Ron was still not in sight.

Grace looked at Joy. "Where is Ron?" she asked.

"He was right behind us a few minutes ago," she replied. Grace watched eagerly as Ron came into the clearing. She rose to greet him. She was still smiling. He was just as tired as she was. He put his back pack on the ground; he was smiling too.

"Have I told you lately that I love you?" he asked.

"I love you too," said Grace.

www.ingramcontent.com/pod-product-compliance
Lightning Source LLC
Chambersburg PA
CBHW071241250626
47163CB00001B/284